D0832965

000000781176

RACE THE WIND

RACE
the
WIND

Lauren St John

Orion
Children's Books

First published in Great Britain in 2013
by Orion Children's Books
a division of the Orion Publishing Group Ltd
Orion House
5 Upper St Martin's Lane
London WC2H 9EA

3 5 7 9 10 8 6 4 2

A catalogue record for this book
is available from the British Library

Typeset by Input Data Services Ltd
Bridgwater, Somerset

Printed and bound in Great Britain
by Clays Ltd, St Ives plc

ISBN 978 1 4440 0270 6

For my sister, Lisa, and in memory of
Morning Star and Cassandra

1

LONG BEFORE ANY of the humans stirred, the horse saw the trouble coming. He stared out into the darkness as two pinpricks of light grew steadily on a country lane where cars rarely passed at 3.35 a.m.

Storm Warning shifted in his stable. His muscles ached, but not unpleasantly. The cheering of the crowd that had urged him on to victory hours earlier still roared in his ears. He had run until his great heart – twice the size of that of a normal horse – had threatened to burst from his chest, yet he'd do it again right now if he could. For if there was one thing he enjoyed more than leaping so high it felt as if he were flying, it was galloping. Storm loved to race the wind.

Impatiently, he jostled the stable door with his

shoulder. In another couple of hours, the birds would begin their dawn song and the sun would outline in gold the leaves of the ancient trees that gave the White Oaks Equestrian Centre its name. Shortly afterwards the stable manager, Morag, a woman he didn't dislike but wasn't particularly partial to either, would arrive with a banging and crashing of buckets, and the grooms would descend, stiff and wild-haired, from their flat above the office.

But that wasn't why Storm was restless. He was hungry for the hour when the girl he adored would come striding across the dew-whitened fields, accompanied by the old woman who smelled of exotic places and had magic, healing hands. When Casey and Mrs Smith arrived at his stable each morning, all was right with Storm's world.

Today, however, something felt different. Felt wrong. As the car drew level with the boundary fence of White Oaks, it slowed to a crawl and turned off its headlights. Like a panther, it crept up the lane, halting outside Peach Tree Cottage. Three dark figures climbed out.

In a pocket-sized upstairs bedroom at Peach Tree Cottage, in the English Garden County of Kent, Casey Blue was dreaming. A smile played on her lips. She was reaching for the Badminton Horse Trials trophy, a magnificent sculpture of three silver horses mounted on a red and black base. Cheers and applause rang out all around her.

'This is a huge achievement for Casey Blue,' the announcer was booming. 'She is the youngest ever winner of one of the toughest championships in world eventing.'

He didn't say that impoverished teenagers from grim concrete tower blocks in London's East End, riding one-dollar horses rescued from a knacker's yard, were not supposed to overcome some of the world's greatest riders to become Badminton champions, but that, Casey suspected, was what he was thinking. And who could blame him? Yet the impossible had been made possible because on the final day, the show jumping round, Storm, who could have been weakened by the gruelling cross-country, had felt strong and sure beneath her.

In the dream, Casey was smiling so widely her face hurt. But as her hands settled on the trophy it was torn from her grip. A flurry of officials surrounded her.

'There's been a mistake,' said one. 'You are not the winner. You don't deserve to be Badminton champion.'

'What are you talking about? Why not?'

'Your father is a burglar. A common thief.'

'He's not!' Casey almost screamed the words. 'Don't say that. He made a mistake once, a long time ago, and he's paid for it. He went to prison and served his time. Haven't you ever made a mistake? And anyway, what does that have to do with anything? This is not about my dad. It's about me and Storm. *We* did the dressage

3

and cleared the cross-country. *We* achieved the times and put the scores on the board. This is *our* life. Isn't that what counts?'

But the officials were walking away, taking the trophy with them, and already the arena had almost emptied. The last stragglers cast disapproving glances over their shoulders.

'We did win,' Casey protested, tears streaming down her face. 'We did win, you know we did.'

An urgent hammering shocked her awake. She lay without moving, trying to separate the nightmare from reality. Had she and Storm won Badminton or hadn't they? Yes, they had. She'd gone to sleep at midnight after an evening of celebration. The trophy was on the kitchen table downstairs, in among the champagne glasses.

She sagged against the pillows, smiling with relief. Now she only had good things to look forward to. Top of the list was the Kentucky Three-Day Event in America. As a result of her Badminton victory, she'd received an automatic invitation. It had put the icing on the cake of the best day of Casey's life.

The hammering came again, and this time there was the sound of footsteps on the stairs and lights clicking on. Still Casey didn't move. It was pitch black outside – 3.46 a.m., according to the clock, and she loathed getting up at that hour, even when she was going to an event.

Besides which, there were plenty of other people to get the front door. Her father was an early riser, as was Peter,

Storm's farrier, who was her ... boyfriend. She had to get used to that word. As of yesterday, he was her boyfriend. There was also Angelica Smith, her sixty-three-year-old coach, who was a bit of an insomniac and was often up all hours of the night, drinking chai tea.

In the kitchen below, the muffled voices grew louder. The stairs creaked. Peter spoke through her door: 'Case, are you awake?'

She sat up, pushing her dark hair out of her eyes. 'How could I not be?'

Light spilled in behind him as he entered. His shirt was unbuttoned, revealing a brown stomach ridged with muscle, hollowing as it dipped towards his jeans. Despite the uncivilised hour, Casey felt her own stomach lurch with longing.

She flushed as the events of the previous evening came back to her. He'd kissed her. He'd told her he loved her. But he didn't look loving now. He looked worried.

'What's happening?' she asked. 'Is it the farmer again? He seems to get a kick out of frightening us from our beds at the crack of dawn. Or is it Morag with some foaling disaster?'

'Casey, you need to get dressed and come downstairs. The police are here.'

'The *police?*' Casey was wide awake now. 'What do they want? Is Storm okay? Please don't tell me he's been stolen.'

'No, Case, they're here to see your dad. I think you'd better come quickly.' And with that he was gone.

Casey flew out of bed in a panic, hands shaking as she struggled to pull on her jeans. Her jumper went on inside out. A thousand thoughts tumbled through her brain.

She'd been fourteen when Roland Blue had been arrested and charged with burglary and assault. The fact that he was the world's most unlikely thief had, in a way, made it worse. The dad she knew had only ever been kind, funny and loving. In court, friends and former employers had lined up to vouch for him as honest and loyal.

But he was also lacking in self-confidence and easily led. His most likeable trait, an infinite capacity for seeing the best in everyone, was not always tempered with good judgement.

A few years earlier, he'd fallen in with a bad crowd. They'd convinced him that a multi-millionaire wouldn't miss a few hundred thousand. He'd agreed to join the gang on a robbery. It was unfortunate that he happened to be knocking the millionaire out with a lamp (the man had woken and tried to kill him with a poker) when the police arrived. In the chaos, his accomplices had fled.

After refusing to rat out his mates, Roland had been left to take the fall on his own. Hence an eight-month prison sentence.

Since then he'd been clean. He'd retrained as a tailor, a job that had become a passion. He was so gifted that he'd hand-stitched Casey's top hat and tails for the dressage at Badminton, embroidering an exquisite rose design on the shoulder and cuffs to remind her of her mother, who'd died when she was two. Roses had been her mum's favourite flower. Casey, who worshipped her dad, flaws and all, could not have been more proud of him.

And now this.

She clattered downstairs and burst into the kitchen. Her first impression was of people frozen in a tableau.

Mrs Smith was leaning against the Aga in her old silk robe, wearing an expression of naked fury. That was the scariest thing of all because very few things in life had the power to upset Mrs Smith's equilibrium. Peter was beside her. He started forward, but Mrs Smith said something under her breath and he stopped mid-stride.

Facing Casey across the table on which the trophy still sat was a large man with blue-black hair and a pockmarked face underlined by several chins. Even unmoving, he exuded a sinister magnetism. His eyes slid over her as if she were of no more consequence than the refrigerator and focused on her father, who wore his rumpled clothes from the previous day.

Flanking Roland Blue were two more policemen – one black and athletic-looking, the other short, stocky and in his mid to late fifties, with an unruly grey mop and pupils the colour of coffee dregs. He had the unhealthy pallor of a man low on sleep and big on caffeine and takeaways, but there was an unmistakable intelligence in his level gaze.

'Detective Inspector Lenny McLeod,' he said, advancing with his hand outstretched. 'These are my colleagues, Constable Dex Higgins' – he gestured towards the black officer – 'and Detective Superintendent Bill Grady. You must be Casey. Apologies for the disturbance. It couldn't wait.'

Casey ignored his hand. Her instinct was to rush to her father's side, but something about the stances of the men discouraged her. 'What's going on?' she demanded. 'What couldn't wait? Leave my dad alone. He's done nothing wrong.'

'That's for a judge to decide,' snapped Grady. 'We have a ton of evidence to suggest otherwise.'

Roland Blue gave a short laugh. 'That's a lie. Evidence of what? That I've been gainfully employed as a tailor and a model citizen? What have you got on me? Did I drop a piece of chewing gum on Hackney High Street?'

Higgins frowned. 'It's a bit more serious than that.'

'A parking ticket? Is that it? Look, if you want a character reference speak to my boss, Ravi Singh. He'll tell you—'

'We already have.' Grady squeezed his bulk into a kitchen chair. 'Can you tell us where you were between midnight and 1.15 a.m. on April 27th?'

A creeping coldness enveloped Casey, as if a winter fog was invading her bones.

'I was at home in Hackney – number 414 Redwing Tower. Speak to Ravi. He and I worked round the clock for two nights running to finish a jacket for Casey. You can see it if you like.'

'Mr Singh did confirm he was with you on the 26th,' said McLeod. 'But he told us he left your flat shortly before midnight when he became too tired to continue. Apparently, you urged him to go home and get some sleep.'

'This conversation is not going any further without a lawyer present, detectives,' Mrs Smith interrupted. 'You've said quite enough. You're making a monstrous error and I'd advise you to leave before you do any further damage.'

Roland smiled. 'Thanks, Mrs Smith, but I have nothing to hide.' He turned to the men. 'So what if I did? Are you going to arrest me for showing concern for a friend?'

'We're rather more interested in a warehouse raid that took place during the hours when you were alone that morning,' Grady said. 'A raid in which a security guard was shot. He died yesterday. That makes this a murder inquiry.'

Roland went white.

Casey rushed forward with a cry, but Higgins grabbed her arm.

'Leave her alone,' Peter said angrily.

Grady rounded on him. 'One more step, boy, and I'll have you down the cells so fast you won't know what hit you. Now stay where you are and shut up.'

Mrs Smith regarded him with dislike. 'We have the

right to call a lawyer, detective superintendent, *and* to be treated with respect.'

Grady heaved himself to his feet and tossed a piece of paper on the table. 'Call all the lawyers you want, madam. Right now, our arrest warrant takes precedent. As for respect ... we save that for thems that have earned it. Dex, read Mr Blue his rights.'

McLeod gave Casey a warning glance and steered her in the direction of Peter.

Constable Higgins intoned: 'Roland James Blue, I am arresting you on suspicion of murder. You do not have to say anything, but it may harm your defence if you do not mention when questioned something which you later rely on in court. Anything you do say may be given in evidence—'

'But this is insane! You have the wrong man. Casey, you believe me, don't you? I'm innocent.'

'I know you are, Dad. This is all just some hideous mistake. We'll fix it, I promise.'

'We most certainly will,' said Mrs Smith.

'Enough time wasting,' snarled Grady. 'Cuff him, Dex. Let's get him to the cells where he belongs.' He almost shoved the pair out into the darkness.

Casey's hands fell to her sides. It was as if someone had tugged at a thread and her whole life had begun to unravel.

McLeod glanced at the trophy on the kitchen table. 'I heard on the news that you won the Badminton Horse Trials yesterday, Casey. The youngest winner in history.

That's some achievement. I'm sorry this has spoiled things. Please understand that we're only doing our job. Uh, congratulations.'

The door slammed shut. The car engine roared and they were gone.

2

C ASEY CROUCHED SO low over Storm's neck that his mane whipped back and stung her face. *Faster,* she urged him. *Faster.*

She knew very well that the last thing she should be doing a mere two days after Badminton was racing Storm flat out on ground slippery from a rain shower, but she wanted to gallop until the events of the past twenty-four hours were as blurred as her vision.

It had taken her until the Monday afternoon to reach her father, who had been held for twenty-four hours for questioning. His words still rang in her ears.

'You're going to Kentucky and that's an order,' he'd told her on a crackling line from a London police station. 'Do you realise that if you won there you'd be in with a chance at the Grand Slam? All you'd need is a victory at the Burghley Horse Trials and you'd be walking into history, Casey Blue.'

Casey's blood simmered at the memory. How could he say such a thing? How could he even suggest it? As if competing meant anything when her sole parent was behind bars for a crime he didn't commit.

'Are you hearing this?' she'd asked Mrs Smith, who was listening on speakerphone. 'An hour ago, Dad was charged with manslaughter, yet he wants me to forget all about it, fly to the US and ride in the Kentucky Three-Day Event. The way he talks, you'd think that being falsely accused of killing a man was as inconsequential as a cold.'

'I'm still here,' her father reminded her. His voice was thick with exhaustion. 'And, yes, I do want you to go to America.'

Mrs Smith shook her head. 'Roland, you're not making any sense. You can't seriously expect us to go to the US and compete when we need to be here, fighting to clear your name? If we leave it to the teenage lawyer you've been assigned by the legal aid people, you'll be sunk.'

'Please, Dad,' Casey begged. 'Be reasonable.'

'Casey, I only have another minute on this phone so I need you to listen carefully. I've no idea why I'm being framed or who is behind it, but the case against me is strong. The police have a lot of evidence. It's manufactured evidence – *has* to be – but that will take time to prove. Time you don't have. The Kentucky event is three and a half weeks away. I want you to give me your word that you'll go there, put this out of your mind and do your very best. My selfish and stupid actions nearly cost you the chance to ride at Badminton. I refuse to let that happen again.'

The payphone cheeped.

'Promise me, Casey ...'

'Dad? Dad, are you still there? Let's see what happens at the bail hearing tomorrow. If the magistrate has any sense, you'll be freed and—'

'What if I'm not?'

The phone went dead.

Faster, Casey urged Storm again, *faster.*

Storm responded like the racehorse he'd once been. His dark silver coat was thunderstorm-black from the earlier deluge and his nostrils flared red as he blasted down the track. Casey clung to his neck, the wind whistling in her ears.

As they swerved through the gate that marked the start of the White Oaks cross-country course, she had a moment of doubt. What if they slipped?

Storm had other ideas. He fought for his head until she set him at the first fence, a small log. It flew beneath him as if it was no higher than a ground pole, but he rapped the next, an easy post and rails. On he flew, spooking at the ditch then doing an awkward show jump that almost unseated her.

The rain started again. It pinged Casey's face like tiny bullets. She tried a couple of half halts but Storm didn't respond. His blood was up and he wanted to run. He was out of balance, galloping long, low and on the forehand. The fluidity they'd achieved at Badminton was gone.

Up the bank they went, skidding off the top and splashing down into a puddle. Casey's stomach was taut with nerves, but there was something about Storm's reckless speed that numbed her pain.

As he soared over the trakehner, Casey had a flashback to their final show jump at Badminton. Suspended in mid-air, she'd caught herself wishing that they could stay there for ever – in that place of perfect happiness. Free from demands of life or the vagaries of love. Free from fear or rejection or hurt. Free.

Barely two days had passed since then. It felt like a lifetime.

Storm took the hedge in his stride and galloped on strongly. Casey's eyes stung with hot tears. The oxer was looming. They were approaching it much too fast, but she didn't have the strength to steady him. His hoofbeats drummed in her ears.

She forced herself to focus. The rain had intensified, obscuring their path, and the last thing she wanted was for Storm to injure himself. One more jump and she'd stop. One more jump and she'd take him back to the stables and face the future, whatever that held.

They tore along the track, spraying mud. Casey tried again to slow Storm, but it was like making a phone call and getting no reply. She concentrated on keeping her hands and body completely still. There was no point in fighting him. All she'd get was a mouthful of mane.

The distance between her and the oxer was narrowing at a frightening pace. Be confident, Casey told herself. Cross-country riding is all about positive thinking. Storm sails over fences three times as hard as this on the circuit.

Her horse's ears pricked. As if reading her mind, he steadied. Out of the corner of her eye, Casey was aware of a slight movement. She turned her head.

A figure in black stepped into their path.

Storm slammed on the brakes. Casey shot from the saddle like a fighter pilot being ejected from a cockpit. She had a split second to think, This could be bad. Then pain shot through her shoulder and everything went dark.

3

'CASE? CASEY, CAN you hear me?'

Casey opened her eyes. Peter and Storm were gazing down at her, raindrops dripping off their noses. It was hard to tell who looked more concerned. She giggled. 'My ears are fine so I guess I'm not dead ...'

The events preceding her fall came rushing back to her and she struggled upright, white-hot agony shooting through her shoulder. 'Is Storm hurt? Oh God, if he's injured I'll never forgive myself. How could I have been such an idiot?'

Reaching up with her good hand, she stroked her beloved horse's muzzle.

Peter's frown was replaced with a grin. He hugged her, causing her to wince. 'Storm's fine. I checked him over while you were coming to. He's broken his reins and is obviously shaken, but his main worry appears to be you. That makes two of us. Casey, you could have been killed. When I drove up in the van, I thought you were ... I thought ...'

With uncharacteristic anger he said: 'Why on earth weren't you wearing a hat?'

But Casey wasn't listening. The face of the man in black, a face out of a nightmare, was emblazoned on her mind. She hauled herself to her feet with the aid of a wet stirrup leather. 'Peter, did you see anyone? When you drove up, did you see a man dressed all in black? Was there anyone like that hanging around the yard? He had this face. This horrible face. He stepped out in front of us and Storm stopped dead in his tracks. That's the last thing I remember.'

'Didn't see a soul. I'm amazed you saw anything at all, the way it was pelting down. Are you sure it wasn't a trick of the light? You may be suffering from concussion. Imagining things.'

'Perhaps,' Casey said doubtfully.

They began the slow walk home, Casey bruised and sore and doing her best to ignore the stabbing needles in her shoulder. She'd refused Peter's entreaties to let him drive her to the yard in the van, because that would have meant leaving Storm on his own until one of the stable girls could fetch him. In the end, Peter led Storm and supported Casey with his other arm.

'Has anyone ever told you that you're extremely stubborn?'

Casey smiled. 'Only every other day.'

She leaned into him. They'd been friends for nearly two years before Peter had told her how he felt about her and she was still quite shy about it, but right now she needed to be close to him. Peter's energy was the opposite of the evil that had radiated off the monster responsible for her fall. Her accident had been no accident, of that she was certain. The man in black had looked directly at her as he'd stepped into her path.

But why had he done it and who was he? A deranged hiker who hated horses? A crazed fan? She thought of Anna Sparks, the girl who'd gone to such brutal lengths to try to beat Casey at Badminton that she was to be hauled before a disciplinary board and probably banned from competing as a result. Much of Anna's dirty work had been carried out by her groom, Raoul. Could Raoul be behind this attack? Was this their way of getting revenge?

The rain had stopped and the fields were draped in golden mist. Had Casey been in any fit state to appreciate it, she'd have thought it romantic. Instead she kept scanning the landscape for the man in black. She knew that she should say something to Peter or Mrs Smith, but what would it achieve? All it would do was upset them. And the police had already shown that they couldn't be trusted.

It was a relief to reach the safe haven of the yard. Morag came over and berated her for not wearing a hat, but otherwise Casey escaped more or less unscathed. She was closing Storm's stable door when Peter put his arms around her. As he gazed down at her, she thought for the hundredth time how good his face was. Not handsome in a movie-star way, but strong and kind. And, of course, he had these melty dark eyes that made you want to ...

'Casey, I couldn't bear it if anything were to happen to you.'

It occurred to her that he might be waiting for her to tell him how she felt about him, which she hadn't yet done. Not in so many words.

More than anything in the world she wanted to say, 'I love you, Peter. Whatever happens, don't let my father's arrest tear us apart.' But somehow the words stuck in her throat. They were selfish. Self-indulgent. With her father in a police cell, how could she even think about love?

Guilt made her lash out. 'Peter, we've only been dating for a day and a half and you're acting as if we're married. Thanks for coming to my rescue but you should probably save your concern for my dad. He's the one who needs it.'

The shutters came down in his eyes. 'Right, of course. Sorry. Well, I'd better go and see Morag. I said I'd shoe a couple of her ponies.'

As his footsteps faded away across the cobbles, Casey shivered. She suddenly felt very alone.

'Fat lot of use you'll be to your father if you end up in traction,' was Mrs Smith's only comment as they sat in the radiology department of the local hospital later that evening, awaiting the results of a CT scan to determine whether or not Casey had a head injury.

'I know I'm an idiot,' said Casey, who had a splitting headache and a shoulder that felt a whole lot better after being clicked back into place by an osteopath. 'Trust me, there's nothing you can say to me that I haven't already beaten myself up about. I'm sorry. It'll never happen again.'

'Well, if it does, at least wear a riding hat,' was her friend's sanguine response.

The doctor who'd given Casey the all-clear had said much the same thing, only using more dramatic language. He'd ranted on about brain injuries and comas and listed gruesome statistics. Casey had nodded earnestly and been suitably contrite. There was no point explaining that in her entire riding life this was the one and only time she'd ever ventured out without a hat, and that there had been extenuating circumstances.

An hour later, she was crossing the darkened car park with Mrs Smith when she saw the man in black lurking in the gloom. He was half-turned away from her, talking to someone in a navy blue Ford.

Casey's pulse rate tripled. 'Quickly,' she said to Mrs Smith, who was fumbling for her keys. 'Hurry. We need to get home.'

With infuriating slowness, Mrs Smith set her handbag on the bonnet of the car where she could inspect it under a streetlight. 'Why the sudden urgency?'

'Just because.' Casey tried to grab the bag and search for the keys herself. 'I mean, Storm has been alone too long and might suddenly have swelled up or something and—'

'Mrs Smith!' shouted a voice. 'I have scoured London for you, to no avail, and here I am in the wilds of Kent and you're the first person I see. Please, Mrs Smith, I need a word with you.'

Mrs Smith froze. So did Casey, who saw her assailant straighten up and look in their direction. A man in a khaki blazer and blue T-shirt – a doctor of some kind judging by his nametag – was rushing across the car park.

'Did you get my letter, Mrs Smith?' he demanded as he neared them. 'It was very urgent. Why have you not responded?'

Mrs Smith snapped out of her trance and plunged her hand into her bag. 'Found them!' she said in triumph. The Honda beeped as she unlocked it. She had the keys in the ignition before she was even settled behind the wheel. Casey dived into the passenger seat. Her door slammed shut as the car shot forward.

The doctor broke into a run. 'Mrs Smith, wait! This is madness. Please, let me talk to you.'

'I get the impression that person would like a word with you,' Casey remarked drily.

The tyres squealed as they sped for the exit. 'He has the wrong Mrs Smith. It's a common name.'

Casey watched in the wing mirror as the man in black and the doctor, throwing up his hands, spun away behind them. She had the sense that both she and Angelica Smith had just dodged a bullet.

'What was that all about?'

'Nothing,' said Mrs Smith. 'Case of mistaken identity.' There was a pause. 'What about you? Anything you'd like to tell me?'

'Nothing at all.'

'Great. Then we'll say no more about it.'

4

DETECTIVE INSPECTOR LENNY McLeod swallowed the last bite of his cheeseburger and tossed the wrapping onto the pile of coffee cups and other rather ripe debris in the well below the passenger seat. It would have taken him five minutes to clean it up, but he left it there because it discouraged his colleagues from riding with him. McLeod much preferred travelling alone.

Left to his own devices he was capable of spending hours daydreaming about the love of his life, Montana. Not the US state, but the bay Morgan mare he'd taken delivery of a few months earlier and visited at her Sussex stable every chance he got. In six months' time, when he retired, he planned to leave his London flat and move to a modest cottage in some remote rural area, where his days could revolve around riding and taking care of his horse.

Once he'd been among the best detectives in the force, ambitious and dynamic, wanting to save the world, but the system had ground him down. So had forty-odd years of plumbing the depths of human nature. Now all he cared about was horses.

It was for that reason that the Roland Blue case had piqued his interest. McLeod had lied when he told Casey he'd heard about her victory on the news. He'd actually watched every spell-binding frame of the Badminton Horse Trials on his television. At the time, he was supposed to be rounding up a teenager who was fencing stolen goods, but McLeod didn't see why he should expend the energy when the boy would get off with only a warning and the very next day he'd have to see the little creep strutting like a rooster outside the school gates.

Instead he'd watched Casey Blue and Storm's epic victory. In the privacy of his living room, he'd shed several tears. It had come as quite a shock when, shortly afterwards, Detective Superintendent Bill Grady, a man McLeod loathed with a passion, had called to say that the father of the winner of 'some big pony event' was chief suspect in the shooting of a now-deceased security guard.

Grady barely knew a horse from a hole in the ground, so that was the first surprise – that the arrogant swine was aware that Roland Blue's daughter was a famous rider. The second surprise was that he'd summoned McLeod. McLeod had always believed the antipathy he felt towards his super to be mutual. Indeed Grady frequently made overloud remarks in his hearing about the 'dead wood' in the department and how it was high time for a 'clear-out'.

Yet when Grady had contacted him at 7 p.m. on Sunday evening, he'd sounded almost eager. 'I know we haven't always been bosom buddies,' he'd begun, 'but I need a man like you on this case, Lenny. I need real experience.'

It was hogwash, McLeod knew, and it had made him suspicious. Grady had been so keen to rush to Kent to arrest Roland Blue that he hadn't even been prepared to wait until breakfast time. He'd wanted them to go swooping in like a TV drama SWAT team when it was still dark. More than that, he'd wanted to be involved.

'Not that I don't trust you and Dex to get the job done, Lenny, but this Blue character might be armed and deadly and I couldn't live with myself if the operation went wrong.'

McLeod had been left with no choice but to participate in the ugly arrest of Roland Blue, and to witness the utter devastation of the girl whose life-affirming performance at Badminton only hours earlier had brought him such joy.

Now something even worse had happened. Her dad had been denied bail.

On the one hand, that was hardly a shock. The case against Blue had a brutal simplicity. On 27 April, there'd been an attempted robbery of a warehouse that stored modern art. It was the kind of art that, in McLeod's opinion, thieves should be thanked for removing, but that wasn't the point. The point was that one of the security guards had been shot by the getaway driver. The prosecution alleged that that driver was Roland Blue.

Seemingly it was an open and shut case. DNA evidence found on a bloodied glove linked him to the scene of the crime. A neighbour at Redwing Tower had witnessed him leaving the apartment with Ravi at around midnight, but was adamant that he still hadn't returned by 1.30 a.m. Roland insisted that all he'd done was walk his boss down to the lobby before going straight home again. The CCTV tape that might have proved which of them was speaking the truth had mysteriously vanished.

That hadn't bothered Grady.

'Guilty as sin,' he crowed as the magistrate banged his gavel and a grey-faced Roland Blue was led away in handcuffs.

McLeod thought that in his entire career he'd never seen a more unlikely murderer than Casey's dad. That didn't mean the man hadn't done it. There were plenty of angelic-looking killers in the world. The difference was, McLeod had seen Roland embracing his daughter after her Badminton win. There'd been tears of happiness pouring down his cheeks as he'd hugged her and Storm.

Hardly the actions of someone who'd recently gunned down a security guard.

McLeod also believed – despite considerable evidence to the contrary – that people who cared deeply for animals, and horses in particular, could not be all bad. Often, they were extremely good.

It was for that reason that he'd decided to do a little extra investigating on his own. Returning with his burger to the court car park, he'd overheard an emotional Casey telling her boyfriend and Mrs Smith that she was going for a walk to clear her head. She'd catch a train later and see them back at White Oaks.

McLeod was well aware that the smart thing to do would be to turn his back on Casey Blue and allow 'justice' take its course, but he didn't hesitate. He started his engine and followed her.

Now McLeod was parked across the street from the Gunpowder Plot pub in Hackney, the East End borough that had been Casey's home until she and Mrs Smith had moved to White Oaks the previous year. It didn't worry him that his car might be spotted, because it was an unmarked, clapped-out piece of junk that blended seamlessly with all the other old bangers on the road. Far more worrying was that Casey had gone into the Gunpowder Plot with a face like thunder. Quite apart from the fact that the place was the haunt of some of London's worst criminals, she was underage.

He was debating what to do about it when she strode from the pub, followed by a tattooed giant of a man. McLeod blanched as he recognised Rick Crawley, aka Big Red, a violent, thuggish brute. Crawley had a reputation for using his forceful charm to win over those weaker, poorer and more vulnerable than himself and get them to do his dirty work for him. Word on the street was that it had been him who'd masterminded the robbery of the dishwasher millionaire, for which Roland Blue had been jailed. Sadly, it could never be proved.

The pair crossed the road and stood so close to McLeod's car that he had to slide down until he was almost horizontal. He could still see Casey in the wing mirror.

She faced up to Crawley, unafraid.

'You are the most gutless man I've ever met. *You're* the reason my father is in jail. If you think I'm going to stand by and let him take the fall for you for a second time, you're mistaken.'

Big Red laughed. 'Oh, yeah. What are you going to do about it?'

'Well, for a start, Dad could tell the police how you and your mate, Foxy, force other people to carry out robberies for you while you get off scot free.'

'Yeah, yeah. Try proving that. As if anyone's going to take the word of a killer.'

'Listen, you miserable lowlife, you know as well as I

do that my dad is a total softie. He couldn't kill anyone if his life depended on it.'

'That's for you to know and the police to find out,' Big Red said sourly. 'And frankly, I don't like your tone. This has nothing whatsoever to do with me. I'm just minding my own business and having a quiet pint. Now if you'll excuse me—'

Casey was furious. 'None of your business? *You're* the one who tried to hire him to drive the getaway car when you were planning the art warehouse robbery. He told me all about it. You claimed it would be a neat, tidy job. "In and out," you said. "No mess, no fuss." He turned you down and this is your revenge – to frame him.'

Crawley strode back and grabbed Casey's wrist so hard that McLeod almost leapt out of his car to save her.

'Now you listen, little horse girl, and you listen good. I might have had a vague notion of doing that job, but that's all it amounted to – a fantasy. I got warned off. Got told that it was more than my life was worth. Told if I pursued it, I'd be supping on river water with the fishes.'

'Who warned you off?' demanded Casey, trying to twist free. 'Who staged the robbery?'

'Don't know. Don't care. And if you fancy being around for your next birthday, you won't care either. Ride your pony and stay well away from this. I'm sorry to hear about your dad. He's a decent sort. I hope things work out for him. But if you show up here again, disrespecting me in front of my mates and hurling false accusations, I won't be answerable for the consequences.'

Releasing Casey so abruptly that she almost fell, he crossed the road and was swallowed by the pub.

Casey stood for a moment trying to restore the blood flow to her wrists. She looked thoughtful rather than frightened. With a last glance in the direction of the pub, she set off down an alley.

McLeod was about to pursue her on foot when his mobile rang.

'What the heck are you doing?' demanded Grady. 'Why aren't you at your desk?'

'I've just seen something interesting. Blue's daughter, Casey, confronted that thug, Rick Crawley, and accused him of framing her father. Why would she do that if her father was guilty?'

'Come on, McLeod. Have you ever known a daughter to believe her daddy was a villain?'

'Trouble is, I'm having difficulty believing it myself. Something about this whole case smells bad.'

The silence went on so long that McLeod thought he'd lost the signal.

'Lenny, I'm correct in thinking that you're retiring later this year, right?'

'Right.'

'After years of sterling service, don't you think it would be a shame if you had to leave the force in disgrace mere months before you're due to collect your pension?'

'Yes, sir, it would.'

'Good. Then we understand each other.'

31

The connection was severed.

McLeod took out his wallet. In the section where most people put photos of their families was a picture of Montana. All his life he'd dreamed of owning a horse like her. Now it had finally happened. Not only was Montana magnificent to look at, she had an amazing nature and was a dream to ride. There was no way he was going to jeopardise that, not even for Casey Blue.

Starting the engine, he drove speedily back to the police station.

5

'TRY AGAIN AND this time take it more slowly,' said Mrs Smith. 'Hold your line. That's a five-stride fence, not a seven-stride one. Sit still and wait for the jump.'

Casey nudged Storm into a canter. For the first time in her life, she didn't feel like riding. Every part of her ached – her left shoulder, her head and her heart. Even her brain. For the past forty-five minutes they'd worked on Storm's show jumping, always a weakness, and things had gone from bad to worse. Casey felt like a beginner who'd been allocated a point-to-pointer at her first lesson.

'I've seen sacks of grain with more style, Casey Blue,' her coach chided. 'Where is your head today? Storm's picked up on that and is behaving like a teenage tearaway at a school camp.'

Storm accelerated towards the oxer and kicked two poles out of their cups before bolting towards the combination and demolishing all three sections.

'It's my fault,' Casey said miserably as the jumps clattered behind her. 'I should never have ridden him around the cross-country course at a flat-out gallop. I've undone months of training in one crazy half hour.'

Mrs Smith stood her ground as Storm came to a snorting halt in front of her. 'Yesterday is history, Casey dear. All we have to work with is the present. Take a break for lunch. I'll look after Storm. When you return, we'll do a few confidence-building exercises.'

Casey slid off Storm, patted him and handed over the reins with a grimace. Under normal circumstances, she would never have dreamed of leaving her coach to deal with her horse, but she was so frustrated she couldn't think straight.

'It's just as well we're not going to Kentucky. At least we'll be spared the humiliation.'

Casey checked her voicemail as she walked across the fields to Peach Tree Cottage. There were thirteen messages on her phone. Seven were from journalists supposedly wanting to interview her about her Badminton victory, but more likely wanting to ask difficult questions about her father's arrest. One was from her Chinese friend, Jin, who'd helped Casey groom and take care of Storm at Badminton, and the rest were messages of congratulation from people on the eventing circuit.

Casey felt like a fraud. It would have been easy to blame her poor performance that morning on stress and sleepless nights, but deep down she knew it was about much more than that.

For as long as she could remember, she'd lived and breathed Badminton. Winning had been the sole focus of her existence. But now that she'd achieved her dream, the enormity of what she'd done was sinking in.

She'd imagined that becoming Badminton champion would put a permanent smile on her face, but she wasn't smiling now. She felt the way she had in her nightmare – that she didn't deserve it. That it was a fluke. That the Badminton trophy belonged to great riders like Mark Todd or Pippa Funnell and not to teenage girls from poverty-stricken, crime-tainted backgrounds. Her riding that morning had been proof of that.

She and Storm had done everything right for one single event. But what if it had been a once-in-a-lifetime thing? What if they were never able to repeat it?

Lost in thought, Casey was tugging her keys from the pocket of her breeches when she noticed that the front door of Peach Tree Cottage was already ajar. It opened with a creak.

'Peter?' she called hopefully, although she knew it couldn't be him, because he'd left early that morning to work at a show in Oxfordshire. She'd done her best to make up for her coldness the previous day and he'd been sweet, but there had been a gulf the size of the Grand Canyon between them when he drove away. They'd been closer when they hardly knew each other.

'See you in a couple of days,' he'd said after giving her a quick hug. She'd wanted to kiss him, wanted to beg him to stay, but she couldn't find the words.

Now she wished that she'd forced herself to say them. As soon as he returned, she'd make it up to him. Her Badminton winnings were in her bank account. She could use them to take him to a special restaurant, or to the coast for a romantic day out. When night fell, they could walk along the water's edge holding hands. With the waves whispering and the moon laying a silver path across the sea, she would finally pluck up the courage to tell him what was in her heart.

The kitchen was empty; the post lay on the mat. Casey picked it up and put it on the table.

'Hello?' she called again. Her skin prickled. 'Anyone here?'

The tidy living room set her mind at rest. The TV, her iPod and the Badminton trophy were all present and correct, which meant the cottage hadn't been burgled. Mrs Smith must have left the door unlocked by mistake.

Casey opened the fridge and took out a ginger beer and the cheese and pickled onion sandwich she'd made earlier. Sitting at the old oak table, she opened the mail. There was an electricity bill, an entry form for an event and, unusually, a hand-delivered letter with her name typed on the front.

Casey took a swig of ginger beer and slit the envelope open with a knife. She thought at first that it was a fan letter from a child who lived locally. The text had been cut out of a variety of newspapers and magazines and glued onto the paper in a haphazard way.

Then the words sank in.

Casey sprang up as if she'd been electrocuted, knocking the chair flying. She twisted around, half-expecting to see a face at the window. Was it her imagination or had an upstairs floorboard creaked?

Stuffing the letter into her pocket, she flew out of the cottage without locking the door and didn't stop running until she reached the barn behind the stableyard. Before she entered, she looked around wildly. Who had done this? Who was out to destroy her and her father? Big Red, or the man with the nightmare face, or someone else entirely? Someone new or someone she knew?

Up in the hayloft, she forced herself to read the letter again. The paper quivered in her hand. There was no 'Dear Casey'. The writer got straight to the point.

If you care about your father you will follow these instructions very carefully. His fate lies in your hands. We hold a piece of evidence – a DVD – that can prove his innocence. To get it, all you have to do is win the Kentucky Three-Day Event. If you fail, he will spend the rest of his life behind bars. Do you really want that on your conscience?

Don't make the mistake of thinking this is a hoax. It is not. And don't worry about who we are or how we will contact you. We are watching you and we'll be in touch when you complete your mission, that's all you need to know.

P.S. If you show this letter to the police or anyone else, your father will never see the sky again. Good luck in Kentucky, Casey Blue.

A combination of rage and despair boiled up in Casey. She didn't know whether to break something or burst into tears. If the threat was real, they were asking the impossible. There was not a rider alive who could guarantee victory in the Kentucky Three-Day Event – not even legends like Mary King or William Fox-Pitt who'd won it in the past. And Casey was hardly at their level. The way she and Storm were going, they'd be lucky if they won a rosette at the local gymkhana.

If you fail, he will spend the rest of his life behind bars ...

Casey gave herself a mental slap. It was ridiculous to get so worked up over a letter that had in all probability been sent by a prankster or a rival. Anna Sparks, her old nemesis, came to mind. She should put a match to it and forget all about it.

38

Don't make the mistake of thinking this is a hoax.

'Casey? Is everything all right?'

Casey got such a fright that she dropped the letter. It floated down to the barn floor, zigzagging like a paper aeroplane. Mrs Smith bent to pick it up.

'Don't touch it!' screamed Casey, descending the wooden ladder so rapidly that she almost fell. 'Leave it alone!'

Mrs Smith put her hands in the air as if she was under arrest. 'Not touching, not touching, promise.' She smiled as Casey snatched up the paper. 'A love letter, I take it?'

'No! I mean, yes. Look, it's private.' Casey pretended a lightness she didn't feel. 'You remember those days, don't you?'

'Just barely. Dinosaurs were still roaming the earth when I last got a Valentine's card.'

Mrs Smith hooked her arm through Casey's as they walked into the sunshine. 'I've taken the liberty of turning Storm out into the field. I thought you could both do with a bit of a holiday. The lead-up to Badminton was quite intense. Since you're not going to Kentucky, you should use this time to rest and regroup before you tackle the season ahead. If that's what you'd still like to do, that is. If you'd prefer to focus your efforts on preparing for your father's joke of a trial, that's fine too. Personally, I don't believe it'll ever get that far. He's innocent and we're going to find a way to prove that.'

'Is that really what you believe? That he's innocent?'

'Not a shred of doubt. He's not perfect, your dad, but he's a gentleman in the true sense of the word. A gentle man.'

The letter burned a hole in Casey's pocket. Should she say anything or not? If there was one person in the world who could be trusted to deal with a dilemma of this magnitude, it was her coach. But she didn't dare. *If you show this letter to the police or anyone else, your father will never see the sky again.*

'I've changed my mind. I do want to go to Kentucky after all. Dad wants me to compete and it's the least I can do for him.'

Mrs Smith stared at her in disbelief. 'But surely he needs you here, supporting him and fighting to free him?'

Casey stepped into the shadows of the tack room before her face betrayed her. 'Why? It's not as if I can do anything, is it? Justice has to take its course. In the meantime, I might as well go to the US and give him something to smile about. At any rate, I need to start training immediately. I'm getting Storm in. His rest is over.'

She slung a bridle over her shoulder. 'I need you to support me in this. I don't just want to compete in the US, I want to win.'

'Is that so?'

Mrs Smith hurried to keep up with Casey as she strode along the path to the field. 'Let me get this straight. Less than an hour ago, you demolished a field of show jumps and declared yourself relieved not to be going to the US because you'll be spared the embarrassment of failure. Now you don't merely want to enter the Kentucky championship, you want to win it.'

'You're always telling me to be positive. That's what I'm doing.'

Casey opened the gate. Her spirits lifted as Storm raised his head. It was two and a half years since she'd rescued him as a half-wild bag of bones from a knacker's yard, paying for him with a US dollar that she'd found in the street, yet she still got a thrill when she saw the transformation in him. He was magnificent.

But was he talented enough to pull off two miracles in little more than a month?

Almost without exception, riders who competed at Badminton took a different mount to Kentucky. Most years they didn't have a choice because Kentucky tended to be held before Badminton, but even when it wasn't few horses were able to follow the huge physical and psychological demands of such a gruelling event with another less than a month later, especially when transatlantic travel and the heat and humidity of Kentucky were factored in. Casey didn't have a second horse. And as brave as Storm was, he did not have superpowers.

He also seemed out of sorts. When she walked up to him, he did something out of character. He turned his back on her and trotted away. When she followed him, he broke into a canter. Casey did several laps of the field and almost had her head kicked off by a Welsh Mountain pony before she was able to coax Storm to cooperate with the aid of a handful of Polo mints. He dragged his heels when she led him to the gate, ears back, tail swishing in annoyance.

Casey felt ill. Theirs was a hopeless cause and she might as well give up now. Her father's freedom would depend on the conscience of the real killer pricking him or her sufficiently to make them come forward and admit the truth.

Once she might have believed that the police would do their job and investigate the case thoroughly. Not that vile, gloating man Grady, perhaps, but his sidekick, DI Lenny McLeod. There'd been something about the way McLeod had conducted himself at Peach Tree Cottage that had made her think there was more to him than met the eye. She'd convinced herself that if anyone could save her father, it was him. But at the bail hearing he'd avoided her. Later, she'd spotted him in the car park, tucking unconcernedly into a burger. She'd lost faith in him then and there.

Mrs Smith kept the other horses back as Casey led Storm through the gate. Her face wore an expression that usually spelled trouble.

Casey grimaced. 'What's up?'

'I've figured it out.'

'You've figured what out?'

'They've got to you, haven't they?'

Casey busied herself with the bridle. 'I've no clue what you're talking about.'

'The gang, individual or whoever has framed your father – they've got to you. That's why you were so afraid I'd see the letter. It's not a love note at all. Let me guess. These people have something – some piece of evidence that will keep your dad in jail for the rest of his natural life unless you do as instructed. If you tell anyone, they'll throw away the key. Is that it?'

Casey thought about denying it, but she knew from past experience that it was useless. When it came to secrets, Angelica Smith had an unsettling clairvoyance. 'How did you know?'

'It's obvious. Your dad has been framed. That much is clear. The question is why and by whom. Either it's because he's being used as a scapegoat to keep someone big out of jail, or someone wants to get to you. Or both. Either way, you might want to tell me what it is that they're demanding. If you're being blackmailed, we can face it together. Two heads are better than one.'

In the privacy of Storm's stable, Mrs Smith studied the letter.

'Maybe it's from Big Red,' suggested Casey, reading it over her shoulder. 'I went to see him after the bail hearing. And before you give me a lecture, yes, I know it was a bad idea. He was pretty mad at me, as you can imagine. Denied any involvement in the robbery. That doesn't mean a thing, of course. Lying comes as naturally as breathing to him. Maybe this is his way of getting back at me.'

Mrs Smith pursed her lips. 'I doubt it. Rick Crawley is far too stupid to have dreamed this up. Look closely at this letter. Ignore the higgledy-piggledy layout of the words, which I suspect has been done deliberately. Much more revealing is the premium-grade writing paper. It hasn't been lifted out of a photocopier. The grammar, punctuation and choice of words also rule out the involvement of uneducated petty criminals. No, we're dealing with an enemy far more sophisticated than that buffoon. As blackmail attempts go, it's so audacious that it suggests the involvement of a person or people in positions of power or influence. It would be a grave error to underestimate them.'

Casey shuddered as she recalled the face of her attacker, twisted and hateful. What if the two events were connected? Briefly, she described how he'd stepped into her path as she flew towards the jump at White Oaks, and her sighting of him in the hospital car park.

Mrs Smith frowned. 'It's unlikely that any blackmailer wishing to remain anonymous would employ a man with such a distinctive face. He may even have been disguised in some way. If the two events are connected

– and doubtless they are – his only purpose was to scare you sufficiently that you'd be more receptive to agreeing to their demands. My guess is you'll never see him again.'

'But what they're asking is impossible,' cried Casey. 'I've been trying to think positively, but the truth is that Storm and I have zero chance of winning in Kentucky. We can barely scramble over a practice jump at White Oaks. Yes, we won Badminton, but you and I both know that there was a lot of luck involved. If these blackmailers had given us some way of contacting them, we could tell them that. They're obviously clueless about horses.'

'No such thing as impossible,' Mrs Smith said calmly. 'Don't believe in the word. And you won Badminton with talent and hard work, not luck. Don't believe in luck either.'

'It makes no difference. Andrew Nicholson is one of the best event riders in history, but he's ridden at Badminton for over three decades without a victory. That proves that even the best of the best can't be certain of winning the greatest championships. And what if Storm gets injured or makes a major mistake in the dressage or show jumping? We might as well give up now.'

'And you're okay to have that on your conscience?'

Casey was close to tears. 'No, I'm not. I just don't see how I can do what they're demanding. I'm a teenager. I've been eventing for less than three years. I can't win to order.'

'Admittedly, it's not an insignificant challenge. From tomorrow, we have just twenty-one days until the Kentucky event begins. Victory would require a radical new approach, as well as a degree of good fortune.'

Casey suddenly became aware that Storm was watching them anxiously. She offered him a Polo mint. To her dismay, he retreated to the corner of the stable. It was something he'd not done since the early days of his rescue. She went over to him and laid a hand on his neck. He trembled beneath her touch. Casey almost snatched her hand away, hoping it was her imagination. Surely their raised voices hadn't disturbed him so much that he was actually afraid. It was a horrible thought that made Casey feel quite ill. She pushed it out of her head and said more quietly: 'We'd need a whole truckload of good fortune, not just a degree. What radical new approach? What would we have to do?'

Mrs Smith leaned against the door and gazed across the fields. At this time of the year they were ablaze with wildflowers and dotted with wobbly lambs. 'Casey, how far are you willing to go to save your father – bearing in mind that there are no guarantees? Blackmailers are hardly trustworthy.'

'To the ends of the earth if I have to.'

'Yes, but what does that mean in reality? How much are you willing to give – physically, mentally and emotionally? How much are you prepared to *sacrifice*?'

'Anything,' Casey said. *'Everything.'*

'Then we have no time to lose. In twenty-one days'

time you will be riding not for glory or fame but for your dad's freedom. For his life. If you are to succeed, every second counts ... Well?'

'Well what?'

'What are you waiting for?'

6

'WHAT EXACTLY DOES this have to do with riding?'

They were in the gritty backstreets of East London outside the Peacock Gym, a brown brick building with a bright blue awning, beneath which crouched a statue of a boxer preparing to punch. From time to time the speeding cars on the nearby motorway flyover sent shadows slicing across the sunlit walls.

'Nothing and everything,' said Mrs Smith. 'We're here because there's someone I'd like you to meet.'

Beyond the entrance was a cafe, where two men were playing chess against a backdrop of boxing photos and autographed photographs of celebrities. Beyond that was a gym that smelled of sweat and soap. The man at the front desk nodded familiarly to Mrs Smith, as though elegant sixty-three-year-old women wearing colourful Indian cottons were a common sight among the weightlifters.

In the centre of the gym, flanked by treadmills and punch bags, was a boxing ring. Casey was riveted by the men inside it. The boxer's skin was red with effort, filmed with satiny sweat. The thwack of his gloves against the trainer's pads was so loud it vibrated in Casey's chest.

She leaned against a pillar, sipping a strawberry milkshake and thinking about Storm. She could think of little else. Overnight she'd convinced herself that his behaviour the previous day had been an aberration. He'd been in a bad mood. But this morning he had, if anything, been worse. Usually, he loved being groomed and made a fuss of. Today he had been restless and fidgety, showing the whites of his eyes.

Casey had said nothing to Mrs Smith. In the back of her mind was the fear that Storm's strange behaviour was something to do with her, and she was too embarrassed to admit that to her coach. If their wild run on the cross-country course had made him distrust her, it was up to her to win that trust back.

That was why she resented being here now. The way Mrs Smith had raved about the place, she'd imagined a gym full of shiny, state-of-the-art equipment and stamina-boosting things like oxygen tents. She hadn't envisaged skipping boxers and walls lined with frighteningly intense training regimes. All she could think was, if I was at White Oaks I could be trying to work out what is wrong with Storm. I could be getting my training on track.

Only one sign resonated with her. THE DIFFICULT WE DO IMMEDIATELY. THE IMPOSSIBLE TAKES A FEW HOURS. A MIRACLE TAKES A LITTLE LONGER. It was a miracle Casey was after.

Pop music competed with the hiss of punchbags and clank of weights. The bout came to an end. The trainer, a thickset black man with dreadlocks, wore a backward-facing red baseball cap. After handing the boxer a towel and a bottle of water, he swung through the ropes and embraced Mrs Smith.

'Always a pleasure, Angelica.'

'Likewise, darling. Ethan, this is the girl I told you about, Casey Blue. Casey, meet Ethan Gage, the best fitness trainer on the planet.'

Casey looked into clear brown eyes in a face that could as easily have been twenty-five as forty-five. She tried not to squeak when her hand was crushed, but it added to her irritation. She wanted to snap: 'I'm not likely to win in Kentucky if my hand is broken.' Instead she said rather rudely: 'The "best fitness trainer on the planet"? That's quite a claim.'

He was amused. 'I'm not the one who made it, Miss Blue.'

'Call me Casey. Do you know anything about horse riding, Mr Gage?'

'Call me Ethan. Not a thing.'

Casey turned to Mrs Smith. 'This is a waste of time. What on earth are we doing here? We should be at White Oaks, working with Storm. Apologies, Ethan, but we need to leave.'

'No worries,' he said easily. 'See you around.'

'Ethan, wait!'

Mrs Smith went after him and Casey could see her pleading with him. His muscular arms were crossed against his chest, his head bowed. She wondered what was being said – how much was being given away. Mrs Smith had insisted that if anyone could be trusted with their secret it was Ethan, but that was when they thought he could help them. Here she was putting Roland Blue's freedom on the line by telling some stranger their business, and it was all for nothing. It made Casey angry. Who cared if Ethan was the best trainer in the universe? If he knew nothing about riding, he was useless to her.

She checked her watch. It was 6.35 p.m. The sooner they were on the train home, the sooner they could get on with figuring out a plan.

The trainer returned with Mrs Smith. He regarded her coolly. 'In a hurry to get to Kentucky?'

Casey took a sip of her milkshake. 'I'm in a hurry to get on with preparing for the championship, yes.'

'So you think you can win it?'

'I'm going to try.'

Ethan scoffed: 'Then I can't help you.'

'I'm not asking you to,' snapped Casey, stung. There

51

was a pause. 'Why not? I mean, why wouldn't you train me?'

'Because people who say things like "I'm going to try" are half-expecting to fail. Because you have twenty-one days to get yourself in a state of extreme readiness for one of the toughest events in the world and you're not remotely serious.'

In the ring, a Thai man in camouflage shorts began kickboxing a sparring partner. Punch, kick. Punch, kick.

'Of course I'm serious,' Casey said angrily. 'I'm not sure what Mrs Smith has told you, but if I don't succeed my father could spend the rest of his life in jail.'

Ethan's hand shot out and grabbed her milkshake. 'Then why are you drinking this? Nutrition affects the hamstrings – very important in riding – and sugar plays havoc with your energy levels and interferes with your body's ability to absorb protein. No protein, no muscles.'

He tossed it into the bin in the corner, above which was a sign: 'RULE NO.1: THE TRAINER IS ALWAYS RIGHT. RULE NO.2: IF THE TRAINER IS WRONG, REFER TO RULE NO.1.'

Casey was livid. 'What did you do that for? I was enjoying it.'

'Let me ask you a question, Casey. What physical attributes do the top eventers need?'

Casey was very proud of the work she'd done to get into shape for Badminton. She stood a little straighter.

'Strong arms and legs, good stomach muscles and core. Great balance. Balance is critical.'

Ethan smiled. 'And you feel you have those things?'

'Four days ago I won the Badminton Horse Trials, one of the biggest three-day events in the world. So, yes, I'm quite fit.'

To anyone watching, Ethan did little more than extend a forefinger and prod Casey's midriff. Yet her legs shot out from under her and she landed flat on her back, winded. It was a few moments before she was able to recover her breath and struggle to her feet.

Ethan made no attempt to help her. 'Sorry about that. However, I think we've established that your leg and stomach muscles are all but non-existent.'

'That's totally unfair. I didn't know that was coming.'

'Is that right? Tell me, when you're riding at top speed over a cross-country course, do you always know what's coming?'

'No, but that's different.'

'How about your balance? Is that any better?'

Casey glared at him. 'Eventing is a sport of three disciplines – dressage, show jumping and cross-country, all of which require fantastic balance. So, yes, mine is pretty good.' She looked around the gym for something she might use to demonstrate. She was determined to prove him wrong.

He rolled a Swiss Ball in her direction. 'Hop on that.'

'What do you mean?'

'Stand on it.'

'It's a ball,' Casey said sarcastically. 'If I stand on it, I'll end up flat on my face.'

'It's easy,' Ethan countered, 'especially if your balance is as good as you claim it is. Watch me.'

With no apparent effort, he sprang directly onto the big silver ball and planted his feet hip-width apart. He then proceeded to do a series of squats and punches as easily as if he were standing on solid ground. Then he tensed his legs and did a backflip, landing as lightly as a cat. Throughout these acrobatics, the ball scarcely wobbled. He grinned as he hopped down. 'Your turn.'

'I said I had good balance. I didn't say I was a circus performer.'

'So stand on it.'

Reluctantly, Casey complied – with predictably comic results. The ball rolled one way and she took off like a hanglider in the other, causing much merriment around the gym. The bodybuilders in particular found it hilarious. She picked herself up again, scarlet-faced.

'You may be a talented rider, but it's clear that you have none of the physical attributes you require for what you're planning,' Ethan told her matter-of-factly. 'How about mental? What does a great rider need?'

Casey was feeling more depressed by the minute, and Mrs Smith was doing nothing to help. 'Focus, I suppose. Courage. Dedication. You need a bond with your horse. Okay, I admit it. You're right. This is hopeless. *I'm* hopeless. My Badminton win feels as if it happened to somebody else in another lifetime.'

She sat on the edge of the boxing ring. 'Look, I don't know what we're doing here. I don't know what Smithy has told you, but we're basically being blackmailed.'

'I know,' Ethan said. 'She told me everything.'

Casey slumped against the ropes. 'Then you'll know that what the blackmailer is asking is not possible. That means my dad's life could be over, and it's all my fault. If I hadn't been so obsessed with my dream, none of this would have happened. If I hadn't won Badminton, we wouldn't have been targeted, I'm sure of it. It's a nightmare situation and I don't know how to fix it. Nobody in the world can guarantee the outcome of a sporting event.'

'No, they can't,' Ethan agreed, 'but think of it this way. When you dreamed of winning Badminton, you were driven by passion and willpower. Now you're in a situation where failure isn't an option. So you have a choice. You can use words like "hopeless" or "impossible," or you can decide that the Kentucky Event is no different from boxers in a ring. If you get your head and your fitness right, you'll smash the odds.'

Without warning, he snatched up a medicine ball and threw it at her. Casey twisted like lightning and caught it.

He smiled. 'Fast twitch muscle fibres. Interesting. That means your reaction times are explosive. Good. We can use that. Train slow, be slow. Train fast, be fast, that's my motto. We'll also need to factor in a bit of meditation to keep you calm under stress. Your fitness and balance we can fix.'

Ethan's gaze had the X-ray quality of Mrs Smith's. Nothing could be hidden from it. Yet after his scathing comments on her physical failings, she was taken aback when he added: 'Courage you have already. No other reason you'd be doing what you're doing.'

'Does that mean you'll train me?' Casey found to her surprise that there was suddenly nothing she wanted more.

'I'd be up for the challenge, yes. Can't stand the idea of this scumbag blackmailer getting away with murder. But I'll only do it on one condition. No excuses. You do what I tell you and you do it with a view to excelling, even when your body is screaming. Agreed?'

'Agreed.'

'When would you like to start?'

'Right now.'

'Are you sure? There's always tomorrow.'

Casey laughed. It was a test. 'No, there isn't. The clock is ticking. I want to start now, this very minute, and I'm not going to quit until I've given it everything I've got.'

7

'I FEEL AS IF I've been kicked all over by a psychotic mule,' groaned Casey as she limped into the yard next morning.

'You might as well get used to it. It's only going to get worse,' Mrs Smith said unsympathetically.

Casey opened the door of an empty stable and collapsed onto the shavings, starfish-like. 'Great. By the time we get to Kentucky, it'll be a wonder if I'm capable of crawling to the start. It took me several attempts to get the coffee mug from the table to my mouth at breakfast time. How am I going to control Storm in my current weakened state? He's getting stronger and stronger. Soon I won't be able to hold him at all.'

'Oh, you don't need to worry about that. From today,

we'll be working without a bridle. Bridleless riding it's called.'

'Bridleless riding? That's funny. Ha ha.' But Casey was talking to thin air. Mrs Smith was on her way to the office.

Climbing painfully to her feet, Casey hobbled across the yard, more Hunchback of Notre Dame than teenage athlete. Mrs Smith was at the sink mixing something green and creamy in a blender loaned to her by Ethan. She poured the foaming contents into a mug and handed it to Casey.

'This will be your breakfast from now on. Ethan's instructions. No more Coco Pops or sliced white bread and jam or whatever it is you live on.'

Casey took a sip. It looked disgusting but tasted okay.

'Natural yogurt, honey, flax seeds, Spirulina – some kind of algae superfood, and raw eggs.'

'Urgh.' Casey spat it into the sink and wiped her mouth. 'No way am I eating raw eggs.' She set the glass down on the counter.

Mrs Smith handed it back. 'Didn't you tell me only yesterday that you'd go to the ends of the earth to help your father?'

'Well, yes, but I didn't think raw eggs would enter the equation.' Casey pinched her nose. 'Okay, here goes, but this had better produce results.'

When it was all gone and nothing terrible had happened, she said: 'There is not a chance in a million that I'm riding Storm with no bridle. In his current mood, he'll race off over the horizon and I'll never be heard of again.'

Mrs Smith perched on the rickety chair in front of Morag's dusty old laptop. 'Come sit beside me. I want to show you something.'

She did an internet search for the American eventer David O'Connor and brought up a YouTube video of him on a gleaming bay horse in a packed arena. Using nothing but a neck rope, he cantered, halted and reined back before clearing several show jumps. Throughout the display, the horse appeared calm and happy. At no time did it speed up or become agitated by its surroundings. Horse and rider seemed to communicate telepathically. Even the neck rope seemed superfluous.

'Wow,' Casey said as the video vanished from the screen. 'That's incredible. I'd love to be able to do that, but it probably takes years to achieve. It also helps if you're a gold medal-winning Olympian like David.'

'It's true that he won gold at the Sydney Olympics,' said Mrs Smith, 'but you and he have something in common. He won Badminton too – back in 1996. He's also won the Kentucky Three-Day Event three times. If he can ride without tack, there's no reason you can't learn to do the same.

'Do you remember how furious you used to get at Hopeless Lane when people hauled at the reins as if they were wrenching at the wheel of a lorry rather than using their legs, seat and voice? Now you're guilty of doing much the same thing. The more you use your reins, the less Storm is going to use his brains.'

Irritated, Casey hopped up. 'Like I said, it's something I'd love to be able to do eventually but there's no time to think about it now. As you keep reminding me, we have twenty-one days to prepare Storm for Kentucky. If anything, we should be looking at using a martingale or a stronger bit. It's the last thing I want, but it might be the only way I'll be able to control him when the pressure is on.'

Mrs Smith followed Casey down the steps. 'As you wish. Only ... '

'Only what?' Casey asked distractedly, looking around. At this time of the morning, the yard buzzed with pupils arriving for a group lesson with Morag or private tuition with Marco and Jessica, the young instructors.

Casey could feel the eyes of the visitors boring into her. One or two looked at her admiringly or called out words of congratulation. Most nudged each other and whispered as she passed. She could imagine what they were saying. *Poor Casey. Haven't you heard? Her ex-con father has been banged up again – this time for manslaughter. Yes, manslaughter. Can you imagine anything more ... embarrassing?*

'I was wondering if you'd humour me with something, Casey?' Mrs Smith was saying.

Casey frowned when she saw that Storm wasn't in his stable. 'Sure. Umm, where's Storm?'

'Oh, didn't I tell you? I turned him out into the field a couple of hours ago.'

Casey, who already felt guilty that she'd slept past Storm's breakfast time, was annoyed. 'Why did you do that? We have tons of work to do. You knew I'd be riding and you saw how hard he was to catch yesterday.'

'Exactly. I saw how hard he was to catch. That's why I thought I'd let him loose in a field, without tack. We're going to be doing some "at liberty" training. It's popular with horse agility competitors. You've seen those shows where dogs do obstacle courses? Horse agility is a similar thing. Horses run freely beside their owner, going over, round and through obstacles, of their own accord. Freedom training fosters trust, the cornerstone of all positive horsemanship.'

'Sounds riveting, but I'm not sure what it has to do with me.' Casey strode past the barn and up the muddy path that led to the lush fields of White Oaks. Storm was in the one furthest from the yard. Frustratingly, he was at the far end. 'If it's all the same to you, I'd prefer to ride Storm around the cross-country course in Kentucky, not run beside him.'

She snatched up a headcollar looped over a fence post.

'It has everything to do with you, Casey Blue.'

There was something in Mrs Smith's tone that stopped Casey in her tracks. She watched her coach make herself comfortable on the top rail of the fence. 'What's this about?'

'Casey, why do you think Storm is pulling so hard at

the moment? Why do you think he doesn't want to be "caught?"'

Casey gave an impatient shrug. 'Because he's super-fit, over-excited and feeling the need for speed. It could also be because he's picked up a few bad habits and is being a bit rebellious and naughty.'

'Naughty? Horses rarely pull or run away because they're being naughty. They do it because humans pressurise them, or ask too much of them, or forget the most crucial rule of horsemanship: always leave your mental rubbish at the gate. Horses pick up on the smallest change in mood or the subtlest alteration in body language. They run to escape from us.'

Casey took some mints from her pocket and pushed open the gate. 'Look, I'm painfully aware that I shouldn't have ridden Storm in anger the other day. I've already told you that it won't happen again. But I love Storm and he loves me. I've only ever been kind to him. There's no reason in the world why he'd want to escape from me.'

Mrs Smith held out her hand for the mints and headcollar. 'Fantastic. Then you'll not be needing those. If you're as in tune with your horse as you feel you are, you'll have no difficulty bringing him over here.'

'Fine.' Casey slammed the gate shut with more force than was necessary and set off across the field.

'Casey?'

She turned reluctantly. *'What?'*

'It's worth remembering that horses hold a mirror up to us. When our behaviour is wrong, their behaviour reflects it. Before you attempt to do anything with Storm, try standing quietly with him. If he leaves, it's because of you.'

Casey kicked at dandelions as she walked. If she were a horse she'd have been tempted to gallop away from her teacher. What was wrong with Mrs Smith? Surely Casey had enough on her plate without also being made to prove that the bond between her and Storm remained as strong as ever. She'd saved him from certain death. They'd won Badminton together. It was ridiculous to suggest that she was making him so unhappy he wanted to get away from her.

But as she walked, Casey's confidence evaporated. She wished she could feel calm, but her mind was scrambled. A kaleidoscope of unsettling images revolved in it. She saw her father's stricken face as he was led away in handcuffs from the court; saw Peter saying goodbye, not meeting her eyes; saw the face of the man in black as he stepped in front of Storm.

She scanned the trees that formed White Oaks' western boundary. One of the things she'd always loved most about White Oaks was the silent majesty of the nearby woods. But from the moment she'd received the letter the secretive trees had taken on a sinister quality. Was the blackmailer concealed among them? Could he be watching her now?

Aware that Mrs Smith was looking on from a distance, she forced a smile and spoke soothingly as she approached Storm. Usually, he stepped eagerly towards her, ears pricked, but not today. Today he stayed where he was and his silver ears went back and forth like small antennae.

To her relief, he allowed her to walk right up to him. She stood quietly, as Mrs Smith had instructed. 'We're okay, boy, aren't we?' she asked him, stroking his neck. 'You and I, we understand each other, don't we? We love each other.'

Storm shifted. Casey's heart sank. He was moving away.

Horses hold a mirror up to us. If he leaves, it's because of you.

In a desperate attempt to make him stay, she grabbed a handful of mane. He jerked away in panic. Before she could say or do anything to repair the damage, he was tearing across the field, bucking as he went. As agonising as it was to admit it, he was escaping from her.

8

THE HUMILIATION CONTINUED on Friday when Peter returned.

Casey had been up since 5 a.m. working with Ethan, who'd agreed to spend four days a week at White Oaks for the duration of their training. They'd started the morning with a 'little something to wake you up'. That was Ethan-speak for whizzing through the woods on a mountain bike, ramping ditches and sloshing through mud, before doing a dozen sixty-second bursts up a steep, bumpy slope, using one pedal only.

'The more fast-twitch muscle fibres you can develop, the quicker your reaction times will be and the more endurance you'll have,' he told her. 'The body has three energy systems: two aerobic – that means with oxygen, and one anaerobic – without oxygen. We need to work them all. Our ultimate goal is to push back your lactic acid threshold so that your body can give a hundred per cent for longer.'

'The only threshold I'm pushing right now is death,' wheezed Casey as she crumpled to the ground outside the caravan. Her thighs felt as if they'd been blowtorched. 'You do know that they require riders to be alive when they enter the Kentucky event?'

Ethan grinned. 'What I do know is that you moan a lot. Here's a skipping rope. Now get on this mini trampoline and start jumping.'

The skipping made the cycling look like a picnic and Casey trembled all over by the time she staggered off the instrument of torture. But Ethan wasn't finished. He then produced a Swiss ball, over which he'd slung two stirrup leathers attached to a central strip of canvas.

'Meet your new best friend. You'll get a proper introduction to the ball tomorrow when we do core work, but I want you to try it out today. From now on, I want you to sit on it any time you might otherwise be on a chair. When you're at the dining-room table or watching TV, for example.'

He rolled the blue ball in her direction. 'Go on. Try it out.'

Casey stared at him. 'Is this a joke?'

Ethan readjusted his backward-facing red baseball cap over his dreadlocks. He was wearing a grey Peacock

Gym T-shirt and his boxer's biceps bulged from the sleeves. His expression told her that he never joked about exercise.

'You want good balance?' he demanded. 'You want to feel as if you're one with your horse?'

An unhappy image of Storm galloping away across the field came into Casey's head. She couldn't imagine ever being at one with him again. When he'd fled from her, he'd kicked up his heels as if he was overjoyed to be free of her, his tack and every other human constraint. The bond that they'd formed over the last two and a half years felt as if it had never existed.

On Mrs Smith's advice they'd left him in the field for the night.

'Let him have some peace,' she'd told Casey. 'He needs some space. Take him food later, but don't try to approach him. Allow him to eat on his own terms and in his own time.'

'I need space,' Casey had retorted, 'but I'm not going to get it. If we don't work this afternoon we'll have lost another precious day from our schedule.'

Mrs Smith sipped her chai implacably. 'Patience, my dear, is a horseman's greatest ally.'

'Okay,' Casey told Ethan now. 'I'll try the Swiss ball. How hard can it be, right?'

'Atta girl.'

She clambered onto the ball rather nervously and put her feet into the stirrups.

'Pick a point on the horizon and focus on that,'

Ethan advised. 'Use your core muscles to balance.'

Unfortunately, Casey's core was not the reliable place she'd once believed it to be. Like a cartoon character skidding on a banana skin, she wobbled frantically back and forth before rolling head over heels. She ended up with the ball on top of her and her feet still in the stirrups. That was embarrassing, but it was nothing compared to the epic humiliation of crawling out from underneath the contraption, beetroot-faced, sweaty and caked in dried mud from the bike ride, to find her new boyfriend falling about laughing.

'Storm not good enough for you any more?' Peter quipped. 'You'd rather bounce around the cross-country course on a big blue ball? Looks like you took the long way through the water jump.'

'Sorry,' Casey said forty minutes later when she'd showered, changed into her breeches and recovered her cool. 'Sense of humour bypass.'

Peter gave her a wry smile. 'That's okay. I deserved it. Note to self: don't make fun of girlfriend when she's muddy and suffering. It took me by surprise, that's all. Why on earth are you torturing yourself like that?'

'I don't exactly have a choice,' Casey burst out, before remembering that Peter knew nothing about the blackmail letter. 'What I mean is, I want to give myself the best possible chance of doing well in Kentucky.'

'*Kentucky?* I thought you weren't going. Isn't it more important that you're here now that your dad's been charged with m— I mean, surely you want to be here in case the lawyer needs to talk to you about the trial?'

Casey gave him a hard stare. 'It's not going to get that far. Dad's innocent, or have you forgotten that?'

Peter flushed. 'No, I haven't forgotten.' He smiled brightly. 'In that case, how about letting me shoe Storm for you? You'll want his feet in tip-top shape for the US.'

There followed the next humiliation.

Mrs Smith, who usually had more tact, said in front of Peter: 'It might be better if I fetch Storm in from the field, Casey. We don't want to upset him any more than is necessary.'

Casey would have raised more objections, but she was secretly afraid that if she went she'd fail and that would be worse. Besides, the morning's gruelling activities had left her as weak as a kitten.

Alone with Peter, she felt awkward and embarrassed. During the course of a sleepless night, she'd rehearsed a whole reunion scene where she'd show him how pleased she was to see him and invite him out for a romantic dinner or day by the sea. After all, it wasn't Peter's fault that her life was in ruins. He was one of the few positives. If she pushed him away she'd lose him, and *that* she was desperate to avoid.

But in the yard her carefully planned words evaporated.

'How was the show in Oxfordshire?' was the best she could manage.

He had his back to her as he fired up the gas forge. 'Good. How's it going here?'

'Good.'

Heaving the toolbox from his van, he turned round. 'Then why is Mrs Smith fetching Storm? What did she mean about you not upsetting him? Has something happened?'

Casey's positive intentions went out of the window. 'Of course not,' she said crossly. 'She's only catching him. It's not rocket science. Maybe she made the mistake of thinking we needed some time alone together.'

Peter's jaw tightened. 'Maybe she did.'

Before anything more could be said, Mrs Smith rounded the corner with Storm, who seemed reluctant but relatively relaxed. To Casey's annoyance, Peter then proceeded to fit him with four immaculate shoes without the slightest difficulty. He had a gift with horses and even the most highly strung trusted him.

As he worked, the muscles bunched and relaxed in his tanned, strong arms. He wore jeans and a faded navy blue T-shirt, his black hair falling over his eyes. Casey forced herself to look away. It would not be a good idea for her to fall any deeper than she already had.

As soon as he finished, she said quickly: 'I'll put Storm in his stable.' If she had her horse in a confined space, she might be able to win him over.

70

'I think not,' Mrs Smith interjected. 'It's the field until further notice. We're in the midst of "at liberty" training, remember? No tack, no restricting his movements.'

The last thing Casey wanted was to have a row in front of Peter. She set off for the field without another word. Along the way she tried talking to Storm and stroking his neck, but he seemed anxious. His ears were back. When she released him, he practically pulled her over in his rush to be free.

Hurt by Storm's inexplicable rejection and still smarting because her boyfriend had handled her horse so much better than she could, Casey was in a black mood when she returned to the yard. Peter was in the driveway, packing up his van. Her anger was gone in an instant. The last thing she wanted was for him to leave. Not that she was about to share that with him.

Leaning against the van, she said casually: 'Going somewhere?'

He avoided her eyes and continued putting away his tools. 'I'd like to stay, Case, but it's probably better if I go.'

'Better for who?'

For the past couple of years Peter and Mrs Smith had been her closest friends, the two people she trusted most in the world. Now Peter felt like a stranger. Casey had to keep reminding herself that he cared about her, that he only wanted good things for her.

'Better for both of us, I guess.' He shut the rear doors of the van. 'For the time being at least. While everything is up in the air.'

There was a knot in Casey's stomach. 'What are you saying? Is this about my father's arrest? Is this your way of telling me that you have doubts about whether or not he's innocent?'

He looked away quickly. 'Of course not. But maybe it's better if you and your dad have the space to deal with this alone. You know, without outsiders like me hanging around. In case things don't turn out the way you want them to.'

'You mean, in case the worst happens and my father does turn out to be a killer after all?'

'That's not what I said. But Casey, you have to admit that the police do seem to have a lot of evidence. That's okay. I'll be here for you no matter what, but maybe you should face up to facts.'

'Peter, you *know* my dad. You can't seriously believe that he's capable of doing such a thing?'

Peter didn't respond. He took his keys from his pocket and stared at them as if they might unlock the secret of the universe.

'You're right. It's better that you go. If you stay I'll only do something stupid like tell you I love you when really I should hate you for saying what you've just said.'

'Casey …'

But she was already walking away. When she heard his van start, a little piece inside her broke. She supposed it was a good thing. Now at least her heart ached as much as the rest of her did.

9

CASEY LEANED AGAINST the paddock fence and buried her face in the sleeve of her sweatshirt. 'Tell me what to do. I'll do anything if only you can show me how to fix this.'

'Are we talking about Storm?'

Casey looked up. Charcoal clouds were moving like tanks across a battleground overhead, but her teacher reclined in a deck chair beside the field as if she were on a beach in the Mediterranean. Mug of chai in hand, she was reading *The Way of the Peaceful Warrior*. Storm grazed in the distance. He had not approached them or even acknowledged them. The change in him was so dramatic that it frightened Casey far more even than the blackmail letter had done.

'Yes, we're talking about Storm.'

Mrs Smith put down her book. 'What if I told you that I could make Storm move his right foreleg without entering the field?'

Casey snorted. 'You're capable of many wonderful things, but that's a bit far-fetched.'

Her friend smiled. She joined Casey at the fence. 'Got your watch on? Good, you can time me. In under five minutes I'll prove you wrong.'

Casey glanced at her watch and then at Storm. After a minute and a half he moved his right foot. She laughed disbelievingly. 'That's a coincidence.'

Mrs Smith shrugged. 'Which foot would you like me to move?'

'Okay, get him to move his left hind leg.'

Forty-two seconds later, Storm did exactly that. Mrs Smith then proved her point by making him move first an ear then another leg, all to order.

Casey stared at her incredulously. 'What are you, a witch?'

'Not at all. Anyone can do it. The point is not to make Storm dance and still less to show that I can control him. I'm merely demonstrating how sensitive horses are to body language and eye contact. Because horses are such large, unpredictable animals, a lot of people believe they have to be dominated with whips, spurs, martingales and severe bits. Yet a single fly can move an entire herd of horses. Same thing with eye contact. You think that Storm is paying no attention to

74

us. In fact, the opposite is true. He's watching our every move.'

'I thought you told me that horses don't like it if you look at them directly because in the wild that behaviour would be aggressive or confrontational.'

'And mostly that's true. For instance, you can bring a galloping horse to a standstill simply by moving your focus from his eye to his shoulder, because in his mind you go from being a foe to a friend. Use submissive body language and the same horse will follow you. All I've done with Storm is apply similar principles. Nothing magical about it.'

She brushed her pupil's fringe from her face. 'Casey, honey, it's not Storm's job to understand you. It's your job to understand Storm.'

'I'm trying, but it's as if he's speaking a foreign language. Less than a week ago, I was fluent in it. Now it's like I have amnesia.'

Mrs Smith sank into her deck chair again, massaging her temples. She'd never have admitted it but her head was killing her. 'Casey, what did you do before you arrived at the field this morning?'

Casey flopped down on the grass beside her. 'Mmm, let's see. First, I was treated to a core session with Ethan, by the end of which my stomach muscles felt as if they'd been roasted on a spit. He also laughed until he cried while I made a fool of myself on the Swiss ball with stirrups. Then my father called and I told him we're going to Kentucky.'

'And that left you feeling how?'

'How do you think? My life is crashing down around my ears. Dad claims to be overjoyed that I'm going to the US, but that's only because he has no idea that his only daughter is being blackmailed – possibly by a psychopath. Peter and I have just ended the shortest relationship in history. Oh, and the horse I adore can't bear to be near me. So no, I don't exactly feel on top of the world.'

'You're surprised that Storm wants nothing to do with you?'

Casey was upset. 'Not you as well.'

'What I *mean*,' said Mrs Smith, 'is that horses are highly attuned to energy. When a rider comes into their space with emotional baggage – it doesn't matter whether it's a great suitcase full of misery or a few trivial frustrations – the horse still wants to flee from it. A lot of times they do what Storm is doing now; they put on armour. Riders tend to interpret that as bad behaviour, or reluctance on the part of the horse to do what is asked of them. It quickly becomes a vicious circle. The more stressed you are, the more stressed your horse becomes and vice versa.'

Casey shielded her eyes against the glare of the pale sky. Viewed in the light of Mrs Smith's theory, Storm's actions made total sense. Ever since her father's arrest, she'd continually approached him in a state of panic, worry or stress. She'd ignored her friend's advice about leaving her 'mental rubbish' at the gate. No wonder he'd retreated into himself.

'Poor Storm,' she said. 'For the past couple of years I've been his place of safety. Now all of a sudden I'm a basket case. I'd run away from me too.'

'But you're not going to,' Mrs Smith said firmly. 'You're going to reconnect with Storm so that we can resume our Kentucky training.'

Casey perched on the edge of a water trough and put her head in her hands. 'How? I don't know where to start.'

'You have to make yourself a pleasant place to be.'

'That'll be tough.'

'Possibly, but that's what you have to do. Loosen the albatross of the past from your neck and look forward. Meditation will help. So will your yoga.'

'And then?'

'Then you have to visualise a bridge running across the field from you to Storm. Go to the middle of that bridge, but no further. If and when he's ready, he'll come to you.'

'What if he doesn't?'

'Casey, until very recently you had the strongest of connections with Storm. Then life intervened and you hung up on him. All you have to do is pick up the phone again and I think you'll find he'll be waiting. The horse is always there. They're always waiting.'

Shortly before nightfall, Mrs Smith crossed the field with a flask of tomato soup, some flax seed crackers, a banana and a blanket. She made no attempt to dissuade Casey from her stated mission of standing on the 'bridge' until Storm decided to cross it, whether that took hours or days. So far Casey had been there since three that afternoon.

'Need any company?'

'Thanks, but no. If Storm ever comes over here, he'll be all the company I need.'

After Mrs Smith had gone, Casey drank the soup and picked at the crackers and watched the last scrap of pink sunset fade into the velvety purple of night. Before entering the field, she'd attempted meditation under Ethan's guidance. She'd been terrible at it. Her thoughts had jack-knifed from Storm to her father to Peter and back again.

Yet when it was over she'd felt calmer than she had done in days. She'd come directly to the field and here she intended to stay until she was 'synchronised with Storm's peacefulness', as Mrs Smith had put it.

The trees were a spiky black line against the sky. They huddled together, sinister and secretive. Casey got goose bumps every time she considered the prospect that the blackmailer – or worse, the man with the nightmare face – might loom from them and strike, but she consoled herself with the thought that attacking her wouldn't serve the blackmailer's purpose. He needed her in one piece to win.

When she'd finished eating, Casey wrapped herself in the blanket and tried to stop herself thinking about what would happen if she couldn't get through to Storm. If he stayed distant. Had it not been for her father's plight, she'd have traded any trophy, future or past, just to bond with Storm again, just to have him love her and trust her the way he had as they'd soared over fences at Badminton.

But as the moon rose and clouds obscured the stars, her spirits plummeted further. There was still no movement from Storm.

She was sinking once more into a depression when she remembered what Mrs Smith had said about being emotionally 'still'. The rubbish in her head was supposed to have been left at the gate. Determinedly, she focused on thinking about positive things.

Not Peter. She refused to think about Peter.

Instead she relived her favourite moments with Storm. Quantum leaps over impossible fences. Lazy afternoons when she'd lain at his feet and read to him. The sensation she'd had during their dressage test at Badminton, when Storm had seemed to float beneath her, when they'd been one perfect unit.

She recalled the morning after his rescue, when the first glimmer of trust had shone in his eyes. She'd arrived at the yard terrified that he might have died in the night and instead his nostrils had fluttered with pleasure and he'd turned towards her, not away from her. For Casey, who'd dreamed of having a horse of her own her whole life, it was nothing short of a miracle.

But the memory that came back to her now was one she'd relived a thousand times in the past week. It was the moment, towards the end of the cross-country at Badminton, when she'd pulled Storm up. He'd been so exhausted that she'd been afraid to continue. Sacrificing her dream had been nothing compared to Storm's health. His life.

But Storm had had other ideas. He'd gathered himself and surged forward, and his courage and willingness to give everything he had for love had bonded them like nothing else.

Now that bond had been broken.

Across the field there was a shimmer, like distant lightning. Casey tensed. Straining her eyes, she could make out Storm's silver outline against the backdrop of the brooding trees. His ears were pricked and he was watching her. She stared back, afraid to breathe. A minute later he took his first step.

The field was empty when Mrs Smith tramped through the damp grass on Monday. For an instant she panicked, but on closer inspection a faint green line across the dew recorded the ghostly tracks of horse and girl.

Storm was in his stable. The door was wide open and he was not tied up, yet he showed no inclination to move. Wrapped in the red blanket and curled up at his feet were Casey and the tortoiseshell cat, Willow, who was Storm's stable companion. They were fast asleep.

Storm stood over them protectively. When Mrs Smith entered, he harrumphed with pleasure, but his black eyes met hers almost in challenge. It was as if he was saying, 'If you dare to wake her, you'll have me to deal with.'

Morag clattered past with a bucket, raising an eyebrow when she saw Casey snoring softly on the shavings. She tapped her watch.

'Casey will have to get her act together if she's to achieve a half-decent result in Kentucky. At this time of the morning she should be working, not napping.'

'She's doing exactly what she should be doing – bonding with her horse,' retorted Mrs Smith. 'That's the best kind of training there is.'

10

DETECTIVE LENNY MCLEOD used a red pen to cross out another day on the calendar marking his march towards retirement and turned his attention to his in-tray. Before him was a towering pile of paperwork, at the top of which was a report on a benefit fraudster who'd played eighteen holes of golf five times a week for four years while claiming a work injury had left him unable to pick up a mug of coffee.

McLeod loathed filling in forms, particularly since the numbing dullness of it freed his mind to think about someone he didn't want to think about: Roland Blue.

Every time he pictured Casey's father sitting in a jail cell he felt ill. He knew that he was committing the cardinal sin of detecting by allowing a case to get too personal, but he couldn't help it. No matter how hard he tried to concentrate on the petty villains in his in-tray, a picture of Casey's face as they arrested her father swam into his head. Something about the situation was as rotten as a box of last year's eggs. It was all too convenient. Every loose end was neatly tied up.

To McLeod, it didn't make sense that the romantic soul who'd hand-stitched Casey's coat and tails for Badminton and embroidered them with roses could later have nipped out to commit armed robbery. Unfortunately, he was alone in the department in viewing this as an inconsistency. Nevertheless, guilt gnawed at him.

The phone rang. He snatched up the receiver, glad of a distraction. 'McLeod here.'

'Lenny, it's Dave from the front desk. I have a visitor for you – name of Peter Rhys. Says he has some important information for you on the Roland Blue case.'

McLeod straightened up. This is what he'd both hoped for and dreaded – someone coming forward with evidence that would conclusively prove the man innocent or guilty. That it was Casey's boyfriend sent shockwaves through him.

Why the lone visit? If it were good news, surely he would have come with Casey.

'Lenny? Are you still there?'

'Thanks, Dave. Send him up.'

Peter took the stairs three at a time. There was a burning sensation in his chest which had nothing to do with the five-floor climb. It had been there ever since he'd driven away from White Oaks.

When the police had showed up at Peach Tree Cottage the previous week with a warrant for Roland's arrest, Peter had tried to refuse them entry. The notion of Casey's gentle, funny, rather hapless father shooting anyone was so ludicrous it was almost laughable. Or would have been had he not been dragged away in handcuffs and charged with manslaughter.

Then came the bail hearing. Listening to the grisly reality of the police evidence – the bloody glove had been particularly upsetting – had shaken Peter to the core.

When Casey had turned cold on him, implying he was smothering her and distancing herself from him so rapidly that she hadn't even bothered talking to him about whether or not she should go to Kentucky, doubts had begun clamouring in his head like a full orchestra. The girl he loved would never have put winning ahead of her jailed father. That Casey was loyal to a fault. She didn't abandon people.

It had suddenly occurred to him that outside of the eventing circuit, he didn't really know her, nor did he know her father. And what he did know of Roland Blue

– a nice man but one with an existing criminal record – did not inspire confidence.

Peter had never intended to fall in love with Casey. He'd tried for a long time to deny it. But in the end her unique combination of shyness and passionate determination, not to mention her storm-grey eyes, tangled dark hair and tomboyish prettiness, had proved irresistible. He'd never met a girl who looked so good in breeches. Kissing her for the first time had been the single best moment of his life.

Unfortunately, opening the door to the police had been the worst. And things had been going downhill at the pace of an Olympic skier ever since.

He thought of Casey saying goodbye to him at the gate of Peach Tree Cottage two days before their row. She'd been half turned away from him, eyes lowered as if they were virtual strangers. There'd been a faraway expression on her face, as if she'd gone somewhere he couldn't follow.

For much of the time he'd known Casey, he'd loved her without ever believing she'd feel anything for him but friendship. After Badminton she'd made it clear that she did. Then her father had been arrested and she'd frozen him out. In his frustration he'd said terrible, unforgivable things. Her response had devastated him. He'd driven away with her words ringing in his ears.

She'd loved him once. Now she hated him and he only had himself to blame.

After his row with Casey, it had taken him two days to come to his senses. It was not until he was shoeing a temperamental show jumper, whose owner remarked stuffily, 'Terrible business, this Casey Blue affair. What a scandal for the Badminton Horse Trials if their champion's father turns out to be a murderer,' that it dawned on Peter that it was not just Roland Blue who was about to become a victim of a catastrophic miscarriage of justice. Casey would have her life destroyed too.

Peter had no intention of allowing that to happen. He felt sick with shame that he'd added to Casey's hurt. She could hate him all she liked; he was going to do everything in his power to help her.

Never in a million years could Casey's dad have killed anyone – he saw that now. The man simply wasn't capable of it. He was a heart-on-his-sleeve kind of person. If he was in the frame for a shooting, it was because someone had put him there.

In an ideal world, Peter would have said this to Casey in person, but he hadn't yet worked up the courage to call her. He'd written her at least twenty texts, including one in the police station reception saying simply, 'I'm sorry. I miss you', but he'd deleted them all before sending.

The top floor of the police station was a curious combination of frenetic activity and apathy. Some officers rushed like roadrunners through the banks of files and computers, barking orders into phones or radios;

others moved as if infected with a collective torpor. They yawned into coffee mugs and sorted drowsily through paperwork.

McLeod was not among either group. Peter found him in a shoebox of an office, hunched over his files. He immediately regretted having come. That night at the cottage, McLeod had seemed different from the other detectives – smarter by a mile and more compassionate. Here he just seemed exhausted.

But as Peter leaned across the desk to shake his hand, he noticed something extraordinary – an oak-framed photograph of a Morgan mare. He lifted the picture.

'What an incredible-looking horse. Just beautiful. She's a Morgan, isn't she?'

McLeod came to life as if someone had flicked a switch. 'You're familiar with the breed?'

'I certainly am. When I was growing up, the owner of the stud next door to my grandfather's farm in Wales was a mad keen Morgan breeder. My dad shod his horses for years until he sold up. We were both sorry to see the Morgans go. They're the kind of horses that get under your skin.'

'Oh, they do. They definitely do.' There was a catch in McLeod's voice and he had to clear his throat several times before continuing. 'Montana has the best nature of any horse I ever came across. Brave and kind. You can see it in her eyes. Quite something to ride too.'

Peter was rapidly revising his opinion of DI McLeod. Any policeman capable of expressing such strong emotions for a horse could not be all bad.

'She belongs to someone you know?'

'She's mine.' McLeod couldn't keep the pride out of his voice. 'She's at livery in East Sussex at the moment, but when I retire we'll be moving ... well, to where I'm not exactly sure, but I'm determined to find a place that allows me to be close to her and take care of her.'

As if embarrassed to have revealed so much to a stranger, he stopped abruptly. 'Enough about the horse,' he snapped. 'Let's get back to business. You have some new information for me?'

Peter sat down. 'I lied.'

The detective's eyebrows rose. 'You lied? About what exactly?'

'I mean, I don't have any information. I only said that so the desk sergeant would let me into the building.'

McLeod moved aside the mountain of files so he had an unobstructed view of the young farrier. 'Then why are you here? Let me remind you, there are serious consequences for wasting police time.'

'Look, I'll be honest with you. Casey doesn't know I'm here. We've sort of broken up.'

'I see. Then what—?'

'I'm here because I want you to know that there's no way her dad could have shot anyone. I doubt he'd do it if his life were at stake. This is a set-up. It has to be.

Somebody is out to get him. Unless, of course, this is not about Roland at all. Have you considered the possibility that it might be about Casey? Criminals target sports stars all the time. Maybe it's no coincidence that her father was arrested within hours of her winning Badminton.'

'That's a very serious allegation, Mr Rhys. I'm assuming you have nothing to back it up. No? That's what I thought. You can show yourself out. I have work to do.'

Peter felt desperate. He was being dispatched having achieved absolutely nothing. Roland Blue would be jailed for a decade or more and Casey's hard-won life, career and happiness would be over. She'd forever believe that Peter had turned his back on her and done nothing to help her.

He leapt to his feet so suddenly that his chair crashed over.

'An innocent man is about to be locked away for a crime he didn't commit, and all you can think about is how soon you can get me out of your office so you don't have to remember that the job of a detective is to detect. It doesn't matter to you that you're about to destroy not just Roland's life but Casey's too, and that they're good people and don't deserve that.'

McLeod got up very deliberately, rounded the desk and righted the chair. He perched on the edge of his desk and folded his arms across his chest.

'Mr Rhys – Peter – I understand your frustration.

Believe it or not, I share some of your concerns. But I promise you I've looked. Like it or not, the evidence is rock solid.'

'Look again,' pleaded Peter. 'Just look again.'

11

CASEY WAS CRAWLING up a sand dune. There were peppery bits of grit in her eyes and mouth and a bucketful of beach in her hair, and her muscles felt as if they'd been through a shredder and reassembled using glue spiced with chillies.

And yet she felt better than she had in days. Even crawling crab-like up a dune the size of Everest couldn't dent her mood, because every metre covered made her stronger, fitter and faster. It also gave her ankles of steel.

But those weren't the only reasons Ethan had brought her to Camber Sands in East Sussex.

'Wait until you see what the dunes do for your balance,' he said. 'Unstable surface, you see. As unpredictable as a horse.'

Casey reached the top of the dune and collapsed, chest heaving. With effort, she managed to raise one painful arm and give a thumbs-up.

There was applause from below, followed by a now-familiar shout: 'You'll thank me when you're in Kentucky.'

'If you haven't killed me first,' she shouted back.

His laughter floated up to her. 'Wimp!'

'Sadist!'

Overhead, the sky looked like a surrealist painting, a garish mix of oranges, yellows and reds. Casey lay for a couple of minutes getting her breath back and drinking in the peaceful sounds of the seaside at dawn: a whisper of waves, the song of the skylarks, the stirring of wind through the deep-rooted marram grasses that hugged the dunes. Even the air was a tonic.

Then she remembered the line in the letter about her father never seeing the sky again and all of her problems returned to haunt her. That was the problem. No matter how hard she tried to focus on Kentucky, the shadowy figure of the anonymous blackmailer was a permanent fixture in the rear-view mirror of her mind.

Casey sat up and pulled a makeshift wooden sled towards her. She banished the blackmailer from her head. Of the many changes Ethan had introduced into her life over the past ten days, meditation had been the most effective. It had taught her to close out dark thoughts before they took root, letting in light or, in this case, the vivid colours of a Camber Sands sunrise.

Levering herself onto the sled, she tipped it over the dune's edge. It shot down the slope at a furious pace before running out of steam a little way onto the beach. Casey was still laughing when Ethan helped her to her feet.

'Had enough? Wanna rest?'

'Why? Are you tired?' Casey teased.

'Will you two sit down and have a coffee and a croissant?' Mrs Smith called from her perch on a folding stool near the water's edge. 'Just watching you exhausts me. Casey, save some energy to work with Storm.'

'With pleasure,' responded her pupil, making a dash for the bag of pastries and taking a bite out of a *pain au chocolat* before Ethan could stop her.

He shrugged. 'Go ahead. Payback time will come later when we do sand sprints, star jumps and burpees. That's when you'll be thinking, If only I hadn't had the wheat that makes me sleepy, or the sugar that makes me moody, or—'

'Okay, okay, you win.' Casey tossed the remnants of the croissant to a hungry seagull. 'But only because you're unbearable when you're smug.'

Ethan grinned as he sat down on the picnic blanket beside Mrs Smith. He took the black coffee she offered him, but blocked Casey's hand when she went to pour some for herself.

'No caffeine for you, young lady. You might as well drink weedkiller.'

'But *you're* drinking it,' she protested.

'How many times do I have to tell you that you have to do what I say, not what I do? Besides, I'm not the one who's competing in Kentucky.'

Casey gave up the struggle for the coffee pot and unscrewed the lid of a flask. 'Mmm, raw egg and algae. Yummy.'

Ethan rolled his eyes. 'Oh, come on,' he said, heartlessly buttering himself a croissant, 'you know you love it.'

The funny thing was it was true. Not about Casey's morning egg-white-and-vitamin smoothie, which she could definitely have lived without, but about the twin training regimes of the ex-boxer and Mrs Smith.

The first four days of working with Ethan had been pure, molten agony. On the third day she'd crawled up the stairs to her bedroom on her hands and knees. But the results were nothing short of astonishing.

A sugar-free diet of high-protein smoothies, vegetable juices and meals of brown rice, fish and vegetables, combined with workouts of military intensity, had left her bursting with energy. After a week, there'd been so many endorphins charging around her system that she'd practically bounced out of bed.

Muscles she never knew existed ached and sometimes screamed as Ethan made her stair-jump with medicine balls, do 'reverse wood chops' with weights, and perform multiple variations of something called 'the plank'. He used terms like 'agonist' and 'antagonist' and spoke at length about lactic acid zones and phosphocreatine systems, most of which went over Casey's head.

It didn't matter. The proof was in the pudding – or as Mrs Smith put it, in the brown rice. It was in Casey's newfound vitality, her lithe, fit body, her rapid recovery rates and, most notably, in her balance. On the rare occasions that she'd ridden Storm over the past ten days, the difference had been striking. She'd felt taller, more connected to him. She had, her teacher noted, flowed with him.

Still, Casey thought, none of it would have mattered had her teacher not done such a fantastic job of organising their trip to Kentucky. Assisted by Jin, the Chinese girl with whom Casey had been friends since their volunteering days at Hopeless Lane Riding Centre, they'd pulled it together in record time. Casey had a shiny new passport with iris recognition. A new suitcase had arrived the previous day.

Most exciting of all were the new clothes and cloud-soft sheepskin-cushioned numnah that had arrived in four big boxes. A gorgeous new rug for Storm was sitting on top of the tack trunk in the living room of Peach Tree Cottage.

Breakfast over, Casey departed for the car park, which despite the early hour was already filled with kite surfers pulling on wetsuits. One ran his fingers through his black, wind-mussed hair as he stood up, and the gesture combined with his broad, tanned, muscular shoulders reminded Casey so much of Peter that the pain that she'd been trying so desperately to block out came rushing back again. It felt as if someone was shaving slices off her heart with a razor.

Abruptly, she turned away. Inside the horsebox, she changed into breeches and a clean polo-shirt, grateful for a temporary respite from the world. When she padded back to the beach barefoot, long boots in hand, she'd regained her composure. She refused to pine over a boy capable of believing her father guilty of a heinous crime. He was gone from her life and she was not going to think about him any more.

Not ever.

Jin was waiting with Storm at the water's edge. Peter and Mrs Smith aside, Jin was one of the few people Casey trusted with her horse. For that reason she hadn't hesitated when her teacher suggested that they bring Jin to Camber Sands for the final stages of Casey's UK preparation. Over the past four days, Jin had spent an hour every morning and evening walking Storm over the dunes while Casey worked out with Ethan.

On each occasion, Casey had followed up by schooling Storm in a bitless bridle. It had been hair-raising, to say the least. Several times she'd felt he was on the verge of running away with her. However, she'd stuck religiously to Mrs Smith's instructions to keep her mind calm and clear, and to yield, not resist, if Storm grew strong. Instead, she was to use her voice and legs to steady him.

Horses, Mrs Smith reminded her, responded to pressure or force with more pressure or force. Their flight response kicked in. The trick was to ask rather than demand that they stop or perform a specific action, and to acknowledge even the tiniest response with an instant release of pressure.

'That's how David O'Connor is able to communicate with his horse almost invisibly. He asks a question in the most subtle way possible and stops asking the instant the horse responds.'

'Rather you than me,' Ethan remarked as he watched Casey mount an excitable Storm with the help of a leg up from Jin. 'He has a mind of his own, that animal. You might as well lasso the wind.'

'It's about trust,' Casey told him, settling into the saddle. 'Storm and I won Badminton because we trusted each other implicitly. When the pressure was on, we were able to put our faith in one another. What's happened over the last couple of weeks has shaken that. I'm doing my best to repair it.'

Before setting off, she asked Storm to stand still and placed a palm on his neck. She didn't pat him because Mrs Smith had a theory that it was something horses endured rather than enjoyed. She simply rested her hand against his silken coat, closed her eyes and concentrated on sending him good energy. The plan was to train him to understand that it meant he should relax and trust her.

Beneath her, Storm gave a violent start. Casey's eyes

snapped open. He was spooking at a kite surfer traversing a far dune.

'That went well,' Ethan said drily, echoing her thoughts.

Casey was annoyed. 'He's not a Shetland pony. He's an ex-racehorse with rocket fuel in his veins and that's the way I like him. We wouldn't have a prayer in Kentucky if he was as docile as an old cob.'

'Chill, girl. I'm talking as a man who prefers his transportation with brakes.'

'Casey will be fine,' her teacher said supportively. 'And horses do have brakes. They merely have to be persuaded to use them.'

As Casey trotted off down the beach and Jin departed to fetch a fresh bucket of water for Storm, Mrs Smith sank onto the rug and massaged her right side with one hand. Most days she could manage the pain with a little aspirin and a lot of willpower, but today it was close to unbearable. The 4 a.m. start hadn't helped.

Even as she watched Casey triumph at Badminton she'd been planning when and how to break it to her pupil that, for health reasons, she'd be reluctantly quitting as her coach. Now it was too late.

Ethan studied her out of the corner of his eye as he poured himself another coffee. Workaholism aside, it was his only vice. Regardless of whether or not it was the nutritional equivalent of herbicide, he had no intention of giving it up. A man who claimed to have no vices at all was not, in his opinion, a man who could be trusted.

'When are you planning to tell Casey?' he asked, watching Storm's silver form gather speed as it moved ghost-like against the waves.

Mrs Smith followed their progress. Further up the beach, a kite surfer was launched into the sky by a smoking breaker. 'Tell her what?'

'Don't play games with me, Angelica. How long have we known one another – a decade? Twelve years? It has to be at least that since you started your home-schooling club for local bad boys, and almost as long since you introduced us to the Peacock Gym. You saved my life, Angelica; there's no other way of putting it. Saved a lot of other wild kids too.'

Mrs Smith shook her head. 'You saved yourself.'

'I made the decision to change, that's true, but you gave me the confidence to do it. You believed in me so I believed in myself. Everything I am today I owe to you, and that's why I'm not going to stand by and let this happen. You're ill, Angelica, don't try to deny it. You hide it well, but you don't fool me. The body is my business.'

She shrugged. 'Maybe I am, maybe I'm not. I did have a few tests, but I burned the results without reading them. What the specialist was suggesting sounded a little scary. I reasoned that what I don't know can't hurt me.'

'Are you mad?' Ethan's eyes were almost black with fury. 'What if it's cancer? What if by leaving it untreated it spreads and becomes terminal?'

Mrs Smith met his gaze unflinchingly. 'Then I'll deal with it after Kentucky. For now, Casey needs me.'

'If Casey knew about this, she'd be devastated. She'd drag you to the hospital right now and demand that you stay there. She'd tell you that no championship in the world, not even one where her father's freedom is at stake, is worth the risk you're taking.'

'And that,' Mrs Smith said firmly, 'is the reason you are never going to breathe a word of this to her.'

The contents of Ethan's mug hissed as they met the sand. 'Angelica, you're gambling with your life.'

In the distance, feathers of spray followed the watery flight of horse and girl.

'Ethan, don't you understand? Casey and Storm, they *are* my life.'

12

THE AIRCRAFT WAS a wide-bodied MD11 operated by Federal Express out of London Stansted airport. It was, in effect, a hollow tube with no seats save a couple behind the cockpit. At the back of the plane were eight boxes, in one of which Storm was now snatching mouthfuls of hay. Intimidatingly, the other stalls were occupied by the mares and geldings of four top riders, including one belonging to William Fox-Pitt.

Casey was glad that most of the pre-flight preparations that day had been done after nightfall and with few observers. The blood in her veins felt as if it had been shaken and stirred and they hadn't even taken off yet. Ironically, she was particularly nervous because nothing had gone wrong. Loading Storm, something she'd been dreading, had been easy. He'd strolled onto the plane like an angel, as if transatlantic flights were an everyday event for him.

Settling him into his stall, where he was sandwiched between two of the finest warmbloods in eventing, Casey had been pink with pride. Physically, at least, her one-dollar horse was a match for any of the champions on the plane. If anything, the mercurial gleam of his coat made the seven bays look ordinary. Best of all, she felt that with each passing day she was rebuilding his trust. He seemed to want to be near her again. She wasn't taking it for granted. A true bond with Storm, a bond that would endure under any circumstance, no matter how traumatic, had to be earned.

It was 9.40 on Tuesday evening. Casey went over her checklist one last time. In the bag tucked under her seat were her wallet, new passport, Storm's export certificate and the trip itinerary from the shipping agent. She'd also brought a trunk containing Storm's blanket, grooming kit and four days' worth of feed, each meal bagged separately and labelled for customs.

Topping up Storm's water bucket with mineral water, she gave him a final kiss on the nose before taking a seat near the cockpit beside the Australian grooms, Annabel and Leanne. They smiled a welcome.

Riders seldom travelled with their horses, partly to avoid the extra expense but mostly because they preferred to arrive at the venue well-rested. By choosing to take the three-day journey with Storm, Casey was adding significantly to the cost of the trip and risking exhausting herself before the competition started. She didn't care. It was worth it to know that someone Storm trusted and could depend on would be at his side every step of the way.

Black rain speckled the porthole windows. The drone of the engines increased by several decibels, ratcheting up the adrenalin flooding Casey's system. She gripped her seat belt and turned repeatedly to look at Storm.

'Relax, girl,' said Leanne. 'Take off will be over before your horse gets it together to be afraid.'

Casey didn't tell her that it wasn't only Storm she was worried about. This flight was the first she'd ever taken and the very first time she'd been abroad. Everything was new to her. Every single thing was, frankly, terrifying.

However, Leanne was right. As the aircraft thundered into the air, the horses snorted and shuffled uneasily, but just as they were starting to get agitated the plane levelled off and the engines quietened.

Casey checked on Storm as soon as the seat belt sign went off. He was tense but gobbling hay, which she took as a good sign. When she returned to her seat, Annabel was talking animatedly to Leanne about her boyfriend troubles. Not wishing to be reminded of Peter, who'd sent her an impersonal one-line text earlier that day – *Good luck in Kentucky* – Casey put on her iPod and tuned her out.

Even with the blackmailer's threat hanging over her head, it was hard not to be excited about what lay ahead in Kentucky. From the moment Mrs Smith had handed her the itinerary from the international shipping agent, Casey had found herself thinking of the trip as a great, if hazardous, adventure.

'The shipping company plan the journey right down to the last detail,' she'd told her father when visiting him that morning in prison. 'The itinerary includes everything from how to pack your tack trunk – all tack and blankets have to be polished and laundered and supplements have to be buried at the bottom – to where to be when. It also has the names of the other horses and their riders, and it's quite surreal to see us listed among them. Storm's going to be travelling in such elite company, I'm worried it'll go to his head.'

He laughed. 'What about you? Any top riders keeping you company on the plane?'

'Nah, just three grooms and a vet. That's okay. If William Fox-Pitt was sitting beside me on the plane, I'd be so overcome with shyness I'd probably crawl into Storm's stall and hide.'

'Casey, Casey, Casey,' scolded her father. 'How many times do Angelica and I have to tell you that you're as gifted as anyone out there and you have the Badminton trophy to prove it. You can go to Kentucky with your head held high. You've earned your place there.'

He grimaced at the prison visit room, where efforts to create a cheerful space were offset by a surly guard and plastic furniture nailed to the floor. 'Forget about all this, and ride for your life.'

I'm riding for *your* life, Dad, only you don't know it, thought Casey as she turned to go. For the hundredth time since she'd received the blackmail letter, she wished she could tell him the truth about why she was going to Kentucky so that he didn't think she was going for purely selfish reasons. But she didn't dare. For a start, he'd instantly forbid her to go. More worryingly, he might flare up and say something to one of the prison guards or his lawyer, jeopardising everything.

She had to walk away knowing that despite the fact that he was urging her to go, he must believe that she cared more about winning championships than about him. Her only consolation was that in ten days he'd know the truth. If she won and if the blackmailer upheld his end of the bargain, that truth would set him free.

The alternative didn't bear thinking about.

As the guard opened the door for her, her father said: 'I'll be with you in spirit every step of the way. You will keep safe, won't you, Pumpkin? I love you. I don't know what I'd do without you.'

Casey had dashed back to give him a hug, giving him her best smile so that he didn't notice she was fighting back tears. 'Course I will, Dad. Storm will take care of me, like he always does, and when we return, this whole misunderstanding – you being in this stupid place – will be cleared up. Love ya. Don't worry about a thing.'

She'd emerged from the visit room to find Chief Superintendent Grady's corpulent bulk blocking the corridor. Up close, he seemed bigger than ever, his skin swarthy and scarred in the fluorescent light.

'What do you want?' she asked rudely.

He leaned against the wall and regarded her with lazy amusement, like a cat contemplating a trapped mouse. 'Don't they teach you any manners on the horse circuit? Or has fame gone to your head?'

For her father's sake, Casey restrained herself from telling him what she thought of him. She folded her arms. 'How may I assist you, sir?'

'I hear you're off to America to compete in some big pony championship. I wanted to wish you well.'

'You did?'

'Yes, I did. Not all policemen are the monsters of popular imagination, Casey Blue. Some of us care about the people we serve and protect.'

'Protect? That's what you're doing for me and my father, is it? Caring for us? Protecting us? Forgive me if I fall down laughing.'

To her surprise, a rueful expression came over his face. 'Casey, I understand that you're frustrated and angry about what's happened to your father, but believe me when I say this situation pains me as much as it does you. We're working as hard as we can to get to the truth about that night. If your father is innocent, justice will prevail. Go to the US and put this behind you. Don't worry about your dad – he's in good hands. Focus on your event. By all accounts, your knacker's yard horse is a force to be reckoned with – as are you, no doubt.' He straightened up. 'That's it. Don't let me keep you. I only wanted to wish you luck.'

Casey was dumbfounded. 'Thanks,' she mumbled, not knowing what else to say. With a sardonic smile and a wave of his hand, Grady was gone.

'What did *he* want?' said Mrs Smith, arriving too late to hear the end of the exchange.

'To wish me luck in Kentucky, apparently.'

Mrs Smith stared after the retreating policeman. 'We'll need it with him in the picture.'

The turbulence started somewhere over Nova Scotia. Casey was swallowing the last mouthful of the meal Ethan had packed for her when the plane bucked so hard that her lunchbox went flying.

'Buckle up,' ordered the flight attendant, emerging from the cockpit. 'We're in for a bumpy ride.'

Until then Casey had thoroughly enjoyed the flight. The grooms told her that unless passengers on ordinary flights paid thousands for first or business class, they were crammed into their seats like cattle. On the cargo plane, she and the others were able to stroll around at their leisure. It was dark outside, so there was no view to speak of, but occasionally Casey saw a starry shower of lights. To while away the hours, she amused herself making up stories about the lives of those far below.

But when the aircraft began to dip and dive, Casey's newfound love of flying came to an abrupt end.

'Ma'am, I need you to fasten your seatbelt,' the flight attendant said more sternly.

Casey stood up. 'My horse is frightened. He needs me with him.'

'And I need you to stay in your seat. From experience, I can tell you that horses make much better passengers than people. They don't know that an aeroplane can crash, you see. They just think they're in a horsebox on a particularly bumpy road. You've been on a few of those, haven't you?'

'Yes, but—'

'Listen to your music and try not to fret. It'll be over before you know it.'

Her optimism proved unfounded. The aircraft began to plunge in a manner that caused even Andrew, the agency groom, a battle-hardened traveller, to look unnerved. Storm squealed with terror and kicked at his stall door. The other horses grew restless.

'You need to shut your beast up,' Leanne said bluntly. 'We can't have him upsetting our horses.'

'Stay where you are,' Andrew told Casey. 'Leanne, leave her alone. The vet and I will deal with Storm. Don't worry, we're used to this.'

Barely a minute later, there was an enraged whinny followed by a crash. Storm reared. Casey flew from her seat. All she could think of was the harrowing scene in *International Velvet* when a horse travelling to the

Olympics goes berserk in mid-air and has to be put down.

'Don't worry, we have no intention of putting Storm Warning down,' the vet reassured her. 'Not unless he breaks a leg or gets loose on the plane or something – which,' he added hastily, 'is not going to happen. However, we do need to get him under control. Fear spreads and we can't have eight horses going mental in mid-flight. We can't even have two.'

Casey almost fell as the floor bucked and swayed. Storm let out an ear-splitting whinny. His neck was dripping with sweat. All except two of the other horses were in a state of high agitation.

'Calm down, mate,' Andrew told Storm, reaching out to pat him. 'Enough of your nonsense.'

Before Casey could move, the horse lunged at him, teeth bared. There was an audible crunch. The groom lurched away, nursing a bloody wound.

'Sorry,' said Casey inadequately. 'He's not used to being handled by anyone but me or my coach.'

'You need to sedate that horse,' Annabel told the vet. 'If Rocket injures himself there'll be hell to pay.'

'You can't sedate him,' Casey cried, as the vet nodded agreement and began filling a syringe. 'Not without my permission. What if you dose him up with something that contravenes FEI drug regulations? What if it affects his performance?'

The vet rapped the syringe smartly to remove any air bubbles. 'There's a risk that traces of the sedative might linger in his system, and I'm afraid that that could well result in elimination. I'm sorry. At this point, we don't have a lot of choice. Your horse is not the only one on the plane. We need to deal with this and deal with it quickly.'

He moved to open Storm's stall.

'Wait!' Casey was almost hysterical as she imagined the catastrophic consequences of not competing in Kentucky. 'Let me try to calm him, please.'

'It's too late. We'll have a lawsuit on our hands if we allow an out-of-control horse to traumatise or injure some of these great champions. Or one of the grooms, for that matter.'

'Let her try,' said Andrew, reappearing unexpectedly. His complexion was flour-white and he was pressing a bloody clump of gauze to his wound. 'We have an unblemished record when it comes to getting horses safely to their destinations and I'd rather not ruin that now. Casey, you have five minutes maximum. If you don't get him sorted, we're knocking him out.'

Casey could have wept with gratitude. 'Give me a book. I'll settle him. Just give me a book.'

'What kind of nuttiness is this?' demanded Annabel. 'Some horse whisperer airy-fairyness? We need to tranquillise him now, not in five minutes' time when he's caused a major disaster.'

The vet ignored her. He delved into his overnight bag and handed Casey Laura Hillenbrand's book on Seabiscuit just as Storm surged forward once again. 'I

110

don't know what you're up to, but whatever it is make it quick. Everyone else, back to your seats. Let's have a bit of peace around here.'

Before entering Storm's stall, Casey took thirty seconds to empty her mind of anything but love. She imagined that she and Storm were in a bubble and that they weren't riding a rollercoaster through the night skies at all, but in his stable at home, on solid ground. When she walked in, she was careful to ensure that her movements were slow and certain even though her heart was thudding madly. Wild-eyed and panic stricken, Storm immediately tried to barge past her.

Casey drew on the experiences of the last ten days and made herself the calm centre of the whirlwind that was her horse. He fussed and fumed and at times almost trampled her in the tight space, but she kept her cool and read. She described the roar from the grandstand and how, in the midst of the noise, Seabiscuit's jockey felt peaceful. The great horse reached and pushed and Pollard bent low over his shoulders and they breathed together. Casey could relate to the feeling and the thought that went through the jockey's mind: *We are alone.*

'It's over.'

Casey emerged from her reverie to find Storm's head buried in the crook of her arm, as if he was a child hiding its eyes from something frightening. The floor of the plane was steady beneath her feet.

'It's over,' the vet said again. 'You'd best return to your seat now. We'll be landing shortly. Well done.'

111

Casey couldn't believe they'd made it. 'Do you mind if I stay with Storm until we're on the ground? He'd be a lot happier.'

'I'm afraid it's against regulations ...' the vet began, but relented almost before the words were out of his mouth. 'In this case, I think, they'll make an exception.'

Casey leaned against Storm's warm shoulder, his mane tickling her face, as the plane swooped into Newark, New Jersey. For the next forty-eight hours she and the grooms would be separated from the horses as they underwent compulsory checks at the Newburgh Quarantine Station. At White Oaks Casey had fretted about that parting, but compared to what they'd been through it now seemed a minor inconvenience.

When the aircraft finally taxied to a halt, she breathed a sigh of relief. It was half past midnight, local time. The first step of her mission was complete.

13

IN THE EARLY hours of Saturday morning, some three and a half days later, Casey was stretched out in a sleeping bag on the shadowed floor of the speeding horsebox. She'd been trying to read a book but she couldn't stop thinking about what lay ahead.

Almost as soon as she'd crossed the finish line at Badminton, she'd moved on mentally to the Kentucky Three-Day Event. Most top riders referred to it simply as the Rolex. It was the only CCI**** in the Western Hemisphere, and since 1998 had been of pivotal importance because, together with Badminton and the Burghley Horse Trials, it made up the Grand Slam of eventing.

In Casey's mind, the Grand Slam occupied almost

mythical status. Considered the pinnacle of achievement in eventing, it had so far been won by only one rider, Casey's hero Pippa Funnell, who also happened to have won Badminton three times. Andrew Hoy and William Fox-Pitt had come closest to achieving a Grand Slam, but no one else had actually done it.

What made Pippa's achievement particularly special was that she'd won the Grand Slam when the cross-country phase still incorporated the steeplechase and roads and tracks and was the ultimate test for both horse and rider. For that reason, Casey spent a lot of time trying to study and emulate Pippa's technique.

But it wasn't Pippa who was on Casey's mind that morning. She was thinking about Mary King, who in 2011, aged forty-nine, rewrote the record books in Kentucky by finishing both first on her home-bred mare, King's Temptress, and second on the flashy grey, Fernhill Urco. She also became the oldest female rider to win a four-star event and the first in the championships' thirty-three-year history to achieve the double.

Casey found Mary's achievements awe-inspiring, but more than that she admired Mary as a person. Quite apart from the fact that Mary was a tremendously likeable, humble woman, who as a verger's daughter came from a background as financially tough as Casey's, Mary's horses always looked as if they were trying their hearts out for her. That was true of most of the top eventers, but somehow it seemed especially noticeable with riders like Pippa and Mary.

No matter how terrifying the jump or how great the pressure at the Kentucky 2011 event, King's Temptress and Urco had radiated a permanent aura of contentment and peacefulness. They were far from easy rides, yet they'd held a mirror up to their rider and that reflection was beautiful. Like Pippa and her horses, theirs was a relationship built on mutual respect and, Casey suspected, love. That spoke volumes. It was their wins and their approach to the championship that Casey planned to draw on when the heat was on in Kentucky.

Stifling a yawn, she stretched her aching limbs. It was clear to her now why most sane riders sent their grooms ahead with the horses, while they flew to Lexington. They would arrive fresh and ready to compete; Casey, on the other hand, felt as if she'd been beaten all over with a large stick.

It wasn't as if she hadn't been warned. Even Mrs Smith had tried to talk her out of travelling with Storm. At the same time, no one understood better than her teacher that the relationship Casey had established with Storm over the past week was critical to the outcome in Kentucky.

Unspoken was the threat posed by the blackmailer. Which was more dangerous – travelling with Storm or travelling without him? Did it matter? Theoretically, it was not in the blackmailer's interests to hurt them, but without knowing who he or she was or why it was that Casey had been targeted nothing was certain.

At Newark Airport, a scary customs official had scrutinised the I DO NOT HAVE A CRIMINAL RECORD declaration on Casey's visa form with bone-chilling concentration. Just when she thought she was going to be thrown into some underground dungeon for the rest of her days for not admitting that her father was currently in prison on manslaughter charges, he flashed an impossibly white grin.

'How about Man United? Are you a fan? Never miss a game if I can help it.'

And Casey had to pretend a massive enthusiasm that she didn't feel for football, all the while thinking what an angel Storm had been, given that his introduction to the US was a Department of Agriculture official with another needle – this one for blood tests.

It was 4.40 a.m. when Casey and the grooms finally offloaded the horses at Newburgh Quarantine Station. For the next two days Storm would be in the hands of quarantine staff and there was not a thing that she could do about it.

The sun was coming up over Lake Washington by the time she'd finally fallen into bed at the motel in New Windsor, New York. When she rose, she felt disorientated and spacey. After the crowds of London and the narrow, leafy lanes of Kent, everything in the US seemed to have been built for a race of giants: the supermarket, the motel bedrooms, the 'parking lot'.

In the diner across the way, a place where the primary food groups appeared to be starch, fat, salt and corn

116

syrup, meals arrived not on plates but on platters that could have fed an African village.

Casey, for whom Ethan had prepared a rigorous diet sheet, avoided sugar and refined flour only because he'd drummed it into her head that success depended on it. Had she been left to her own devices, she'd have had no hesitation in joining the grooms as they tucked into the pancakes and warm maple syrup with gusto. Instead she ate two plain yogurts, a banana and three tablespoons of flax, sunflower and pumpkin seeds.

'Why don't you relax and enjoy yourself?' urged Leanne, who was doing her best to make up for her harsh words on the plane. 'Let your hair down. We're stuck here for two days. Come into New York City with us and do the tourist thing. We're planning a trip to the top of the Empire State Building.'

Casey had always dreamed of visiting Manhattan, the birthplace of her American mother, but now was not the time. She was not in the US to have fun; she had a job to do. If she lost focus now, she could forget about finishing first.

While Leanne, Annabel and Andrew went shopping and sightseeing, Casey swam, worked out and dozed when she could. She also bought food for the journey to Kentucky, so she didn't have to resort to takeaways. The itinerary had described in vivid detail the 'long, cold and uncomfortable drive in the horsebox' that lay ahead. A sleeping bag, pillow, torch, iPod and reading material were, it said, necessities.

As the drive neared its fourteenth hour, Casey was glad she'd brought all of those things. Climbing stiffly from her sleeping bag, she went over to Storm. He whickered with pleasure, stretching towards her to breathe in her scent.

'If I'd known that absence would make your heart grow so much fonder, I'd have done it sooner,' Casey told him.

As if in reply, he shoved her with his nose. He had suffered no obvious ill-effects from his gruelling journey. If anything, he seemed positively energised by his experiences.

'That often happens with the intelligent ones,' Andrew had told her. 'They're inquisitive, you see. For them, a change is as good as a holiday.'

Casey strapped on her watch. It was 6.42 a.m. In less than twenty minutes they'd reach the Kentucky Horse Park, their final destination. She went to the window and looked out. They were in or near Lexington, home to some of America's greatest racehorses. Pristine white fences lined the famed bluegrass pastures, where thoroughbred mares, foals and yearlings grazed in the honeyed glow of the early morning sunlight. Pretty painted barns made each farm unique. Casey couldn't believe how immaculate they were. Not a blade of grass was out of place. It was like riding past the film set of *Secretariat*.

Her fear of what lay ahead momentarily subsided and she felt a rush of pure adrenalin. Mrs Smith had bought her the DVD of Mary King's one-two in Kentucky. Over the past ten days, she had watched Mary ride the cross-country course most nights before she went to sleep and she'd committed every stride to memory. From time to time she allowed herself to slip into a daydream where there was no blackmailer. Where the letter had been a hoax. Where she and Storm were free to compete and go for sweet victory in Kentucky on their own terms.

After all, that one threatening note aside, there was actually zero evidence that the man existed.

Storm whickered again and pawed the floor. Casey tore herself away from the view and gave him a couple of Polo mints. 'Yes, I know, you're desperate to get out and galloping. Believe me, so am I. But you'll have to be patient. When we arrive, a Department of Agriculture vet has to unseal the horsebox and check you in. After that I'll be free to settle you into your new stable and give you a nice breakfast.'

'You do know that he doesn't have the faintest clue what you're going on about, don't you?' Leanne said wryly, overhearing her as she tended the Australian horses. 'The only part of that sentence he's likely to have understood is the word breakfast.'

Casey didn't bother to respond. As far as she was concerned, Storm understood every word. With a non-committal smile, she opened her tack trunk and pulled out the blanket. Beneath it was a typed note:

DON'T THINK YOU CAN ESCAPE FROM US, CASEY
BLUE. WE'RE WATCHING YOU 24/7. ONE FALSE
MOVE AND YOUR FATHER IS HISTORY.

Casey slammed the lid closed. The last time she'd opened
the trunk had been at 3 p.m. the previous day, shortly
before the horsebox departed the Newburgh Quarantine
Station. Two government officials, the three grooms and
the driver of the horsebox aside, it was impossible for
anyone else to have accessed it. That meant that one of
those people was either working with the blackmailer or
was the blackmailer.

At the back of Casey's mind lurked the conviction
that her tormentor was the man with the nightmare
face who'd caused her fall. That it might be a rival rider,
aided and abetted by one of the grooms who'd pretended
to befriend her, was spine-chilling.

'What's wrong?' demanded Leanne. 'Has something
been stolen? Have you had some bad news?'

'Nothing's wrong. I ... I've just realised I've run out of
Polo mints.'

The Australian girl laughed. 'Is that all? Here, have a
packet of mine.'

14

ON AN UNSEASONABLY cold, rain-sodden day in East London, Lenny McLeod swerved up to the kerb and slammed on his brakes unnecessarily hard, almost catapulting Peter through the windscreen. He didn't apologise. The risk he was taking by including the boy in the investigation and having him ride in the passenger seat like a fellow officer was so great that he didn't see why he should apologise for his driving as well.

'Redwing Towers,' he announced, 'Casey's childhood home. Soon to be vacated by her father if the super has his way.'

He turned off the wipers and glistening pellets of rain blurred Peter's view of the grey block, less a tower than an overgrown concrete block. Built in the sixties, it had been the subject of several valiant attempts by Hackney council to spruce it up but still resembled the London division of Alcatraz.

Up close, it was no better. The sad patch of lawn that fronted it was unkempt and littered with cigarette butts. The foyer was decorated with graffiti. As they passed the open lift, Peter caught a whiff of spilled beer and other things he preferred not to think about.

It was impossible to imagine Casey growing up in this hellish place, let alone emerging with enough faith, hope and courage to become one of the hottest young stars in the sport of horse trials. And now, through no fault of her own, everything she'd worked for was about to be snatched away.

He'd persuaded himself that that was why she'd gone to Kentucky – to put on a brave face and prevent her career from imploding. He didn't want to think about the alternative – that Casey cared more about winning than love. That she'd gone to the US because competing in Kentucky was more important to her than the father she'd left behind in a prison cell.

McLeod was watching him closely. 'You've never been here before, have you? Does it make you think less of your girlfriend?'

Ex-girlfriend, thought Peter, though he didn't say so.

His heart felt numb, as if a part of him was dying. 'No, it does the opposite. It makes me think more of her.'

122

'Anyone coulda took it, couldn't they?'

The caretaker had barely risen off his chair when they'd entered and was once again slumped in his seat, as if the effort of standing was beyond him. 'I mean, we get all sorts here. Well, you seen some o'the rabble out there. You should be busying yourself arresting them, not harassing an upstanding citizen like myself.'

'We're hardly harassing you,' said McLeod. 'We're merely suggesting to you that it seems coincidental that the one tape that could prove Mr Blue innocent has vanished without trace.'

'Don't blame me, blame the council,' the caretaker sniped. 'I do me best but I'm not going to stand guard over the place twenty-four seven. It's not a fortress. I reckon some kid nicked the videotape to record his favourite TV show or some such.'

Dragging the few strands of hair he still possessed over the top of his shiny head, he used the other hand to gesture towards the dust-streaked chaos of video cassettes spilling tape, old newspapers, miscellaneous household appliance parts and tools. Two small, equally grimy televisions displayed a sequence of flickering black and white images of various parts of Redwing Tower.

He took a slurp of tea. 'Typical of the police, isn't it? A whole building packed with teenage gangsters and the kind of people who'd raffle their own grandmother if it got 'em a night's beer money, and you go after one of the few decent residents in the building. Sure he did a burglary once but he never profited from it, did he? He did his time. How long are you going to make him pay for it? And you coppers wonder why folks at the tough end of society can't stand the sight of you. Well, you don't do nothing for us, do you?'

Peter admired McLeod for keeping his patience. Unable to bear the stale air in the office a moment longer, he stepped out into the courtyard. The rain had temporarily ceased, but water still gurgled and sang in the gutters.

He wondered where Casey was and what she was doing. There'd been a snippet in the *New Equestrian* about how she'd turned down the offer of a free business club ticket on British Airways in order to accompany Storm Warning on the plane to the US, committing herself to nearly four torturous days of travel.

Asked if that was wise, given that she was already disadvantaged because she was taking Storm rather than a fresh horse to Kentucky, she'd responded that eventing was not only about winning. 'Storm and I are a partnership. I couldn't live with myself if something happened to him because I chose to travel in luxury. If he needs me, I want to be there.'

In spite of everything, her comment had made Peter smile. Now that was the Casey he knew.

There was a sharp sting on the back of his neck, quickly followed by another on his jaw as he turned.

Two small objects dropped at his feet. He was amused to see that they were frozen peas.

He was scanning the labyrinth of passageways that enclosed the courtyard in a bid to locate the sniper when two further peas smacked him in the forehead. Half-irritated, half-impressed by the audacity of the marksman, Peter held up one palm. 'Bet you can't hit this!' he called to his unseen assailant.

Seconds later a pea pinged off his hand. Peter laughed out loud. 'Great shot!'

On the fifth-floor balcony, a small face appeared momentarily at the railings. It flashed a grin.

'Everything all right?' asked McLeod, appearing at his side. The face disappeared from view. 'I'm going up to the fourth floor to talk to the couple who claim to have witnessed Roland Blue leave his flat shortly before midnight on the night of the shooting and not return for several hours. They've already been interviewed, but that doesn't prove anything. Funny thing about investigation; people's memories often improve with time.'

Peter waited in the communal corridor outside a flat that smelled of chip fat. The television was blaring, but the strident voice of the woman who lived there, Mrs Block, carried clearly as she talked to McLeod.

'Course 'e did it. Not a doubt in my mind that 'e's guilty. I told you that 'e was a bad sort all along, didn't I, Bob?'

The response, if there was one, was drowned out by an escalation of the drama on the TV.

'The moment 'is daughter started getting rich and famous and in the newspapers with 'er fancy horse, it went to Roland's 'ead like strong wine. It was all Casey this, Casey that. Got above 'is self, 'e did. Already done one burglary, so 'e thought 'e'd do it again, didn't 'e? Obviously wanted a few bob so 'e could move into some posh mansion with Casey and have stables at the back. Never did trust 'im further than I could throw 'im. As for that daughter, full of airs and graces. Soon as she started doing well, she were like the Queen when she came round 'ere, weren't she, Bob?'

Rage, an emotion that seldom surfaced in Peter, bubbled up in him. How dare this hideous woman lie about Casey and her dad, two of the most down-to-earth, humble people he knew.

He turned away and leaned over the peeling railings. A wave of nostalgia for the peace and space of his grandfather's farm came over him. Nature was his home. Cities made him claustrophobic at the best of times and Redwing Towers, with its damp-stained walls, poky spaces and twitching net curtains made him want to run for his life.

Directly opposite him, on the far side of the courtyard, was 414, the flat where Casey had grown up. If he closed his eyes, he could imagine her coming home from an evening's work at the riding centre she and Jin called Hopeless Lane. She'd have been wearing the shapeless breeches and pink, bargain-basement polo shirt in which he'd first seen her, and walking in that tomboyish way

126

of hers that was part shy and part swagger. Friends of his considered her plain, but to Peter she'd always been quite heart-stoppingly beautiful.

He suddenly realised that he was gripping the railing so hard that the blood had drained from his hands.

'Anyway, it's all coming back to haunt 'im now. Like I told that other detective, Don Alexander, Bob and I, we saw him leave the building with his friend at about midnight. They were carrying a couple of bags. I'm sure about the time because we were watching a re-run of *Total Wipeout*. 'E never came back – not for hours. First Bob was 'aving a fag and then I joined 'im, and then we got talking to our neighbour, Margie Adams. The whole time I was watching to see what 'e was up to, but he never came back. Didn't see 'im till he came out to get the newspaper at nineish the next morning.'

McLeod said. 'How can you be sure that he didn't come back while you were standing in the corridor? You were talking. You might have been distracted.'

'Not likely. Did I tell you Bob was a chain smoker? So's Margie. I kept 'em company and we set the world to rights. But all of us were watching like hawks to see what he was up to. We finally turned in at about 1.30 a.m. because old misery guts upstairs was complaining about the noise.'

Another frozen pea hit Peter on the head. He lifted his hands in mock surrender.

A thin arm waved at him from the stairwell. Peter

went. If he stayed where he was, Mrs Block would only annoy him even more.

The tiny assassin darted up the steps, summoning him to follow. It was only when he reached the floor above that he saw what he'd imagined was a boy was in fact a girl with short black hair, a thin pale face and green eyes.

Peter hesitated near the open door of what he assumed to be her home, reluctant to talk to her unless a parent was nearby, but she gestured him over impatiently. She was clutching a white pad. On it, she drew a series of precise dots and pointed across the courtyard at number 414, Casey's home.

'I don't understand.'

Sighing dramatically, she connected the dots. A centaur with a bow and arrow emerged from a remarkably rendered section of stars.

Again, she pointed.

He followed her gaze. 'I'm not sure what you mean. Is this your star sign? Are you a Sagittarian?'

She made a huffing noise and wrote CENTAUR on the pad.

Peter laughed. 'Oh, I get it. Casey is like a centaur – half-girl, half-horse. That's brilliant. She sort of is, you know.'

The girl put down the pad and presented him with her catapult. He was trying to refuse it without offending her when he was shoved violently aside. A woman scooped up the girl and cradled her. 'Get away

128

from her,' she screamed. 'Leave us alone. How dare you!'

The girl started to cry.

Peter was alarmed. 'I'm so sorry. I … I … She was shooting frozen peas at me. I— I'm with the police.'

The woman's face cleared and she put the girl down, giving her a squeeze that brought a smile to the child's face almost instantly. 'Sorry, angel. Mama was worrying for nothing as usual. Would you mind fetching me a glass of water, sweetheart? Bring one for this nice policeman too.'

As soon as the girl was gone, she turned to Peter. 'Apologies if I seem like one of those slightly deranged tiger mothers. You have to be, living here. Especially when you have a child who enjoys targeting visitors with frozen vegetables. I'm Kate Watson, by the way.' She looked him up and down. 'I must say, you don't look like a cop.'

'I— err, we have a new team on the case now,' he stalled. 'We're reviewing the evidence.'

She glanced around and lowered her voice. 'Well, you might want to review the evidence of those awful Blocks. They've been telling everyone in the building that they're helping the police with their enquiries. They're lying, you know.'

Peter gave her his full attention. 'You mean they weren't in the corridor on the night they say they were?'

'Oh, they were there. Twice, I went down and appealed for them to be quiet for the sake of Myra and our elderly neighbour. They laughed in my face. That's the sort of people they are.'

'They might be loud and rude, but that doesn't necessarily make them liars.'

'No, it doesn't. But what I want to know is how they managed to see Roland's comings and goings from the fourth floor stairwell. That's where they smoke, you know. Not the corridor outside their flat.' She pointed to a sign on the wall. 'No smoking in public areas. Of course, the stairwell is a public area too but they don't seem to see it like that.'

Peter's blood quickened, but all he said was, 'We'll look into it.'

'I hope something comes of this now,' said Kate as he turned to go. 'Ever since I lost my job and we were forced to move in here a year ago, Roland has been one of the few rays of light in our lives. He's truly one of the kindest men I've ever known. And Myra, who loves animals, worships Casey. You'll do your best to help them, won't you?'

'Yes, we will. I can promise you that.'

Thanking her and Myra for the water, he went down the steps. He had no difficulty in finding the smoker's corner. It was a nook just off the landing screened by grey slats that offered glimpses of the street. At the foot of one of the slats some enterprising soul had inserted a biscuit tin with a hole cut in the side. It was crammed with cigarette butts. But that wasn't what caught Peter's attention. What struck him was that while it was possible to see the doors of almost all the fourth-floor flats on the front and left-hand side of the building, the corridor and doors on the right side, where 414 was located, were invisible.

McLeod rounded the corner. He was annoyed. 'There you are. I thought I was going to have to send out a search party.'

'I think,' Peter said, 'you need to take a look at this.'

'So what happens now?' Peter asked excitedly when they reached the car. 'Now you have proof that Casey's dad didn't do it, how soon do you think you can get him out of jail?'

McLeod started the engine. 'And why should he be released? Because a couple of eyewitnesses proved to be unreliable? Welcome to my world. No, we need cold hard facts. Don't believe everything you read in the papers about being innocent until you're proven guilty.'

Peter was crushed, but more than that he was furious with himself. How could he have been so naive as to think that he could play at being detective and solve the mystery in a single morning? In his head, he'd already leapt ahead to the phone call where he told Casey that, far from believing her dad was guilty he'd had a hand in setting him free. He'd imagined her joyous reaction.

He punched his thigh. What an idiot he was.

McLeod gave him an amused glance. 'What's with the fit of gloom? Thanks to you, we've just scored our first breakthrough in the case – quite a coup for an amateur.'

'I thought you said that what I found proves nothing.'

'I said it didn't prove that Roland was innocent. But the fact that a detective as high-ranking as Don Alexander interviewed the Blocks but didn't bother checking their story tells us something interesting.'

'What's that?'

'That we're looking in the wrong place and worrying about the wrong person.'

He put the car into gear and moved out into the traffic. 'From the beginning, this case hasn't made sense to me. I couldn't understand what would motivate Casey's father to take part in a robbery during the most important week of his daughter's life, and I've been mystified by some of the decisions taken internally about the investigation. Now I'm starting to believe that you're right. This is not about Roland at all. This is about Casey.'

Peter felt a chill go through him. He'd suggested it as a possibility, but he hadn't really believed it. 'Go on.'

'Don Alexander is one of the most talented young detectives in the force and all the signs are that Grady is personally grooming him as his successor. He's ambitious and has a reputation for having expensive tastes, but I doubt he'd risk his career by getting involved in anything dodgy. At the same time, I have to wonder why it is that two of the highest-ranking detectives in the force are making it their mission to rush this case through and send a man to jail for life. My gut tells me that this has something to do with his famous daughter, but I can't for the life of me think how or why.'

'What if Casey is being blackmailed for some reason?' suggested Peter. 'I mean, one minute she was adamant that under no circumstances would she leave her father to go to Kentucky, and the next she was not only going but desperate to win. When I questioned her decision, she almost bit my head off.'

'It's a possibility, but who would be blackmailing her and why? And what possible connection could Don Alexander have with the case? He's not even working on it. As far as I know, he's out of the country on honeymoon.'

'Any idea where he's gone?'

'Long Island, New York, I believe. Normally, I wouldn't have taken the slightest bit of notice, but he was boasting about being invited to ride champion Arabs and dressage horses at the estate of his rich in-laws. I have to confess that I was green with envy. Before Don became a detective, he was in the Queen's Horse Guards, based at Buckingham Palace. That's where he got his taste for the high life. Show jumped and evented at quite a high level.

'On paper, he and I have quite a lot in common, at least where horses are concerned, but for some reason I've never liked the man. I've no idea why. He's always been perfectly pleasant to me, and last year he offered me a couple of tickets to the Burghley Horse Trials when he couldn't—'

He veered off the road and braked hard. For a long time, they sat in silence.

'That's the connection,' Peter said.

'Yes, eventing is the connection.'

'Peter, I need you to understand something. This is not a game. If we pursue this line of investigation, if I shine a light inwards at my own force, it could be deadly dangerous for you and get me thrown out of the service without a pension. In short, the ramifications could be catastrophic. No one would blame you if you walked away now, least of all me. But I need you to make a decision. Are you in or out?'

Peter didn't hesitate. 'I'm in.'

McLeod nodded his approval and for a second the young Welshman caught a glimpse of the determination that had once made McLeod one of the most effective detectives in the force. The car spluttered forward. As Hackney's Murder Mile clamoured around them, the unlikely team only had one thing in mind: saving Casey Blue.

15

O N   T H E   O T H E R side of the world, the subject of
their concern was riding a counter canter beneath
an electric-blue sky. It was barely 9.30 in the morning,
but already the air was so close and thick it was like
breathing in hot cotton. Casey's polo shirt was sticking
to her back. Storm's silver coat was streaked with foil-
coloured rivulets.

There was a buzz in the air, a palpable thrill that
raised Casey's adrenalin levels until the blood practically
fizzed in her veins. At twelve hundred acres, the
Kentucky Horse Park was significantly smaller than
Gloucestershire's Badminton Park, and yet it was
designed on such a grand American scale that it felt
many times larger.

Casey's favourite section so far had been the Breeds Barn, which was home to three dozen different varieties of horse, including a couple of exquisite doe-eyed Morgans. When Casey visited, a feathery-footed Clydesdale was being shod by the resident farrier. She'd caught herself comparing the man unfavourably to Peter and had given herself a mental slap.

The day after Mrs Smith had arrived, looking more weary than Casey might have expected after her flight, she'd insisted that they take a tour of the park. Casey had gone along under sufferance and thoroughly enjoyed herself. The International Museum of the Horse was the highlight, but it was also fascinating to see the working horse farm, Hall of Champions and the fine schools, show rings and other facilities.

In the four days since her arrival, Casey had walked around in a state of awe. Perhaps it was the sunshine, but everything and everyone seemed to have acquired an extra coat of gloss. Horses that Storm had competed against and beaten now seemed impossibly sleek and muscular. Jockeys she knew to have suffered similar struggles to herself looked as glamorous, sophisticated and expensively attired as if they were modelling for an equestrian edition of *Vogue*.

The strange thing was that she was wearing the same clothes they were. As a consequence of her Badminton victory, she had money in the bank and a sponsorship deal to wear the most stylish shirts and breeches in the business – brand new Ariat long boots and breeches, Kingsland polo shirts, and smart Pikeur shirts for the dressage and show jumping. Yet compared to these shiny happy people on their specially bred warmbloods, she felt poorly turned out and shabby.

Deep down, she knew that her clothes had nothing to do with it. Losing Peter, seeing her dad in jail and being hounded by the blackmailer had taken a big bite out of her confidence.

Remembering Ethan's advice, she did her best to turn the thought around in her head. If a part of her always remained the 'donkey-van girl' who'd started out on the circuit in charity shop breeches, riding a one-dollar horse, perhaps that wasn't a bad thing. Self-satisfaction bred complacency. Adversity was what kept career athletes hungry. And hunger was an essential ingredient in the drive to win.

'Sharpen up that canter and then collect him,' encouraged Mrs Smith. 'Good. Keep your leg around him so he doesn't lose impulsion. You want him thinking forward, which is going to earn you more points. No, no, no, don't override it. You started well, but you used too much leg and pushed the quarters out. Bring him back to a walk.'

As Storm slowed, Casey expelled a breath in a frustrated hiss. 'If I can't get this right in practice, how on earth am I going to get it right tomorrow, when the pressure is on and I'm in an arena being watched by thousands of people?'

Her teacher smiled. 'Believe it or not, you are improving.'

Casey was sceptical. 'Are you sure? Because sometimes it feels as if we've been making the same mistakes for the past two years. As hard as I try, I always seem to do too much of this or too little of that.'

Mrs Smith hopped down from her perch on the railings and came over to Storm, reaching up to rub his forehead. She was coolly attired in pale blue linen. 'Casey, the trees that give White Oaks Equestrian Centre its name, they're over five hundred years old and about a hundred metres high. Have you ever seen them grow?'

'Uh, no.'

'And do they grow?'

'Obviously, they do.'

'Same thing with horses and riders. There's a constant process of learning, but on a day-to-day basis it's mostly invisible. It can take six months to achieve one tiny result. That's what I learned when I was competing at dressage. The best dressage riders and trainers – people like the British Olympic gold medal-winner Carl Hester or the German legend Klaus Balkenhol, think nothing of spending five or more years finessing certain techniques.'

'That's all very mystical and wonderful,' said her charge, 'but I don't have four or five years. In four *days'* time I have to win this championship. Somehow. Don't ask me how.'

Even as the words left her mouth, Casey felt a

corresponding weakness in her arms. Through kinesiology, a muscle-testing procedure which aimed to balance the body physically, emotionally and nutritionally, Ethan had demonstrated that a negative thought instantly sapped the strength from her muscles.

'Stand with your arms outstretched at shoulder height, palms down, so that you're in the shape of a cross. Great. Now think of one of your favourite memories. When I push down on your right hand, I want you to try to resist the pressure.'

Easy. Casey recalled flying over the last show jump at Badminton to the deafening approval of the crowd, and then slipping off Storm into the arms of Peter, Mrs Smith and her father, the three people she loved most in the world. The commentator was so excited that his voice had gone up several octaves. In the midst of her happy daze, she'd had a sudden vision of him floating off to the heavens like a helium balloon.

But it was the way she'd felt that was most unforgettable. The blood in her veins appeared to have been replaced with liquid joy.

'Amazing,' was Ethan's verdict as he pressed down on her right hand. Casey had no difficulty resisting him.

Then he asked her to think of her worst memory. She recalled sitting in court, watching her father being taken away in handcuffs, distraught. She thought of Peter's face, hard and unrecognisable as he'd questioned her father's innocence.

At the slightest touch from Ethan, her arm dropped to

her side as if it was made of lead. A paralysing weakness had taken hold of her.

Thinking of that now, Casey pictured herself riding strong and proud into the arena for her dressage test next morning. She'd be wearing the top and tails that her father had made for her, and Storm would float beneath her like a horse from a dream.

'You won't win by thinking of the event in its entirety,' Mrs Smith said as they worked on their rein-back just in front of her. 'You can only do it by being in the here and now. Do your very best at every moment and whatever the outcome, you'll have no regrets.'

Casey didn't argue. As a former dressage champion, few people were better qualified to give her advice than Angelica Smith, reputedly one of the finest riders in the world in her day. And there was no doubt that Mrs Smith's methods, viewed as eccentric by many of their fellow riders, were working. After nearly two weeks in a bitless bridle, Storm's responses to even the lightest aids with his regular bridle had undergone a startling change. He moved better. He carried his head better. Most of the tension had gone from his neck.

Best of all, he'd stopped fighting Casey and wrenching her arms from their sockets. The day before they'd done no work at all. Mrs Smith had insisted on it. She'd said that Wednesday should be about nothing but fun. That meant a long hack across the park's emerald pastures, past spotty Appaloosas and Quarter horses with coats like copper fire or molten gold.

As he stretched out across the Kentucky turf, Storm had felt loose and springy. He was fascinated by everything. When they passed the Breeds Barn, his ears were so pricked they were practically touching.

Since he'd suffered not a single ill effect from his journey, Casey had come to the conclusion that Andrew, the shipping company groom, had been right. Intelligent horses relished changes of scenery and fresh challenges. For them, it was boredom that was the real killer.

She asked Storm for an extended trot.

'Try that again,' called Mrs Smith. 'Think of it as changing gears. If your medium trot has too much energy then your extended trot is not going to look a lot different. The judges want to see a clear transition from one stride to the next.'

Casey and Storm did it three more times, each time better than the last. They finished the session with a serpentine and a halt.

When Mrs Smith came over, she was glowing and not just because of the searing Kentucky heat. 'You won't get everything right tomorrow; it's that simple,' she told Casey. 'The most important thing is to approach each movement individually and then put it behind you as rapidly as you'd move on from a poor fence.

'Success in dressage is about two things: focus and quality. Think about Piggy French at Badminton in 2011. The last movement of her test, a canter down the centre line followed by a halt, moved grown men

141

to tears. She earned several nines and one perfect ten from the ground jury. People tend to focus on the flashy moves, but doing the simple things exceptionally can bolster your score dramatically.'

She hugged Casey and gave Storm his mints. 'Now go and have some fun. Personally, I'd encourage you to go wild and eat a vast plate of pancakes and maple syrup or maybe drink a milkshake or two. Tomorrow is important but it's tomorrow. Remember what I said and stay in the here and now.'

As Casey and Storm left the school, a woman on the top floor of a nearby building lowered her binoculars. She was in her late fifties and by no means the beauty that had once made her the toast of high society on New York's Long Island, but her high cheekbones and shimmering mane of auburn hair still turned heads, just as her position as one of America's leading equestrian judges still commanded the respect she craved.

Sixteen months earlier, her privileged lifestyle had almost come to a humiliating end when her hedge-fund manager husband had dropped dead at a dinner party. He'd eaten a strawberry, which the hostess had inexplicably added to a salad and to which he was violently allergic. It was not until a week later that Elizabeth Vale-Edwards discovered that thanks to a series of disastrous investments, her late spouse had left his family bankrupt and owing millions.

Faced with ruin and the repossession of her estate and precious Arab horses, Elizabeth had confided in her daughter. Isabelle had in turn confided in her fiancée, a British detective who'd proved astonishingly useful since she and her mother had struck up a conversation with him at a polo match in the UK.

Ordinarily, Elizabeth considered policemen to be among the lowest of the low and would not have dreamed of allowing Isabelle to marry one, but Don Alexander was no ordinary cop. He was charismatic, charming and had the manners of an aristocrat. More usefully, he was connected and had several unusual talents. Thanks to these special gifts, Elizabeth was well on the way to securing her family's future and regaining her place as the reigning Queen of Long Island.

The door opened behind her. 'Pleased with my selection?'

For a moment, her mask slipped and she turned on her visitor with a snarl. 'What are you doing here? What if someone sees us together?'

Don Alexander smiled his famously irresistible smile. 'Calm down. I was careful to avoid the cameras. In the unlikely event that someone recognises me I could always say that I'm here in an official capacity – investigating the doping of a champion horse or something. Trust me, Lizzie, it's all going to be okay.'

Ordinarily Elizabeth loathed being called Lizzie,

but Don's British accent made the name sound like a character out of a Jane Austen novel. 'All right, but you can't hang around long. We have work to do. I will admit that Casey Blue is your most inspired choice yet. Rarely have I seen an athlete work harder and it's clear that her horse has exceptional range and talent.'

'So you're no longer concerned about her youth?'

'I'll be honest with you, I did question the wisdom of targeting another teenager at first. Too mercurial and unreliable. But you were right, as usual. They're very pliable and obsessive. That Slovakian tennis player we went after at Wimbledon last year came through with flying colours.'

'Unfortunately, Miss Blue is by no means a sure thing. Her inexperience could be a big problem. What I'm hoping will be in our favour is that her coach is top class. If anyone is capable of ensuring that the kid survives the dressage test and is up among the leaders after the cross-country phase on Saturday, it'll be Angelica Smith. She's a former dressage champion, you know.'

'I still don't see why you're refusing to judge Casey in the dressage,' Don said peevishly. 'Surely, that would be the easiest way to skew the results in our favour? All you have to do is give her lots of eights and nines.'

'Because, my dear Don, that would be the fastest route to prison. Anyhow, if I did judge her I'd be so conscious of not being seen to favour her, I'd probably go too far in the other direction. No, it's better that she's marked by someone objective. I have a replacement lined up. What about your side of the deal? The evidence against the girl's father. Is it solid?'

'It's about as solid as a matchwood raft in a tornado. It wouldn't stand up to the scrutiny of a blind mouse. For instance, it won't take long for someone to figure out that the glove that we produced in court was stolen from the evidence bag used in Roland Blue's old burglary case. We simply put a drop or two of the security guard's blood on it.

'But don't panic. Grady's put old Lenny McLeod on the case. He's just months away from retirement. He was a great detective once, but nowadays he's burned out and more obsessed with this Morgan mare he owns than solving crime. He's not going to do anything that might jeopardise his pension. The man barely leaves his desk. Even if he does and finds that the evidence is – how shall I put it – flawed, he's unlikely to do so before Sunday evening. That's all the time we need. Once Casey has done what we need her to do, we plan to release her father ourselves. That's the beauty of this scheme. Nobody gets hurt.'

'Except for Roland Blue, who gets to spend a month in a cell accused of a crime he didn't commit.'

'Since when did you develop a conscience?'

Elizabeth ignored him. 'The money is organised, right? You've placed the bets?'

Don flicked an imaginary speck of dust off the sleeve of his white shirt and made himself at home on the corner of a desk. 'Relax, my fair lady, we're good to go.

Our contact in New Jersey managed to get the note into Casey's tack trunk as we discussed, so she'll be primed and ready to do our bidding. Stop fretting. Nothing to do now but let the fun begin.'

She laughed. 'I do enjoy your turn of phrase, Detective Inspector Alexander. All right, I'll quit worrying and look forward to seeing my bank balance on Monday.'

16

C ASEY WARMED UP for day two of the dressage
on Friday with the words and music of the telecast
she'd heard a couple of hours earlier booming in her ears
like a movie soundtrack.

'Three days in the Bluegrass State . . .' the announcer had
been saying dramatically as she tugged on white breeches
and buttoned her crisply ironed shirt. 'The premier
event on the American equestrian calendar – the Rolex
Kentucky Three-Day Event – featuring the precision of
dressage, the first of three distinct disciplines, where horse
and rider must master intricate ballet-like movements . . .
The controlled fury of the cross-country . . . and then the
final test, stadium show jumping, racing against the clock,
conquering the obstacles, all to become a champion.'

Pulling on her shiny new long boots, Casey had smiled at the bit about the ballet-like movements. Aside from one dressage test rehearsal, Storm's preparation over the past three days had been a mix of conditioning sprints and what Mrs Smith called 'play'. Using methods inspired by horse agility training, she'd made Casey run ahead of Storm and have him follow her over jumps and over, round and through a series of small obstacles. The pair had looked less like dancers than characters from an absurd comedy sketch.

Still, like almost all of Mrs Smith's ideas, it seemed to have worked. Storm was more content than Casey could ever remember him being at an event and that in turn helped her. Breathing deeply and rhythmically, she asked him for an extended canter, concentrating on getting as deep as she could into the final marker. The points, Mrs Smith maintained, were in that extra stride. It was that attention to detail that had helped Mary King win in Kentucky. She'd refused to leave a single point on the board.

On the far side of the warm-up area, Mrs Smith tapped her watch. In preparing for the dressage, they'd left nothing to chance. Casey had gone over her test until she could do it in her sleep (she'd been doing a five-step rein-back when her alarm went off), and they'd timed the distance to the stadium to the second. Too early and Storm might get unsettled during the wait. Cut it too fine and her nerves might communicate themselves to him.

As she moved towards her teacher, the silk lining of Casey's coat and tails brushed coolly against her wrists and brought a smile to her tense face. Putting on the coat her father had made for her with his own hands, a navy blue one with roses embroidered on the shoulder and cuffs in memory of her mother, made her feel close to him. It eased the guilt she felt at being away from her dad. It was as if he and her mother were with her and had cast a protective shield over her.

Unfortunately, all the preparation in the world could not change the fluke of fate that caused Sam Tide's horse to shy violently as he left the stadium, throwing him so hard against an advertising hoarding that he broke an arm and two ribs. There was a lengthy delay while paramedics attended the scene and an ambulance took him away, and further confusion when Elizabeth Vale-Edwards, a member of the ground jury, was taken ill and a replacement judge had to step in. Casey's start time of 2.10 p.m. was moved first to 2.20 p.m. and finally to 2.35 p.m.

It was while she was waiting and growing increasingly nervous that Scott McHendry, a groom who was a close friend of Peter's, approached her. At the sight of him, Casey's heart contracted painfully. The three of them had often hung out together on the circuit. He congratulated her on her Badminton victory and they talked a little about who was and wasn't likely to do well in Kentucky.

He'd just launched into an extended monologue on the merits of the motel breakfast when Casey did something

149

she had been counselling herself not to do all along. She asked about Peter.

Scott's eyes did the sideways and upwards flick of someone about to lie. 'Haven't seen him in ages. You'd probably know better than me. I – uh, shouldn't you be warming up?'

Instantly, Casey was suspicious. 'Scott, what's wrong? Where is he? If you know something, you need to tell me.'

'Casey, this isn't the time. You're about to do a dressage test. Let's talk about it later.'

'NO!' said Casey, so loudly that another rider turned to glare at her. 'Tell me now. I need to know.'

Scott was squirming with embarrassment, sweating with it. 'Look, Case, I'm the wrong person to ask. You should be talking to Peter.'

'Come on, Scott. I don't have a lot of time.'

'Okay, okay. Yesterday I had a shoeing issue and I tried calling Peter, but he hasn't answered his phone in like three weeks. So I rang his dad. Evan told me that Peter's taken an indefinite leave of absence because he's in London helping some detective with his enquiries.'

Casey paled. 'What enquiries?'

'Something to do with the charges against your father, I think. Look, I'm sorry you had to find out this way. I told you that this wasn't the best place ...'

'And it isn't,' said Mrs Smith, who'd arrived in time to hear the end of the conversation. She shot him a freezing glare. 'Good day to you, Mr McHendry.'

150

Scott scuttled away, stumbling and almost falling in his effort to escape.

Casey was a wreck. There were tears in her eyes and she was shaking. Picking up on her distress, Storm began to prance. Mrs Smith did her best to soothe him.

'How could he? Is this Peter's way of getting back at me – helping the police dig up evidence against my father?'

Suddenly, nothing else seemed important. Not the blackmailer and his demands. Not the dressage test still to come. Not winning the trophy on Sunday. She sagged in the saddle.

Mrs Smith reached up and took Casey's gloved hand between hers. 'I don't suppose it's occurred to you that he might care so much for you that he's taken leave from his job to help the police find evidence that might free your father.'

'Casey Blue,' interrupted the steward, 'you're up next.'

Casey had a split second to decide what to think. Was the boy she knew and loved capable of doing something so cruel to hurt her? Or could he be doing what Mrs Smith suggested – trying from afar to help her?

She moved into the stadium in a trance, barely able to respond as Storm snatched at the bit. Despite the delays, the stands, bright with the green and gold banners of the championship's sponsor, were packed. The vastness of the space was intimidating, and the charged atmosphere even more so. As she entered, she caught a glimpse of herself on a huge screen.

Storm was all over the place. He spooked at a camera and almost unseated her. Pulling herself together, she sat deep in the saddle and rode past it again to allow him to take a good look at it. Mrs Smith had been emphatic on that point.

'I've seen more than one great test ruined because the horse took fright at a flower box or something equally inconsequential. Before you enter the arena, take him past everything that looks even vaguely threatening.'

Casey knew she was right. If they were to achieve anything at all, Storm needed to be focused and comfortable.

A memory flashed into her head. Her, Peter and her father, sitting in the kitchen late on the night of her Badminton victory. The friends who'd shared in their celebrations had left, and Mrs Smith had gone to bed. Peter was holding Casey's hand under the table and they were all laughing. At some point, her father had got up to make them mugs of hot chocolate and Peter had used the opportunity to steal a kiss from Casey and look at her. *Really* look at her. And the expression she'd seen in his eyes had taken her breath away.

In that second she knew, just absolutely knew, that whatever Peter was doing, he was doing it because he cared. A feeling that was almost supernatural, of being flooded with warm golden light, swept through her. She laid a palm on Storm's neck. Over the past twenty-one days, it had become their signal. It was her way of saying to him, 'Trust me. Put your faith in me. I promise I'll make everything okay.'

They entered the arena in a collected canter, Storm keyed up, but responsive. Their halt was close to perfect. Casey saluted the ground jury and gave them a radiant smile. Proceeding in a collected trot, she tracked to the right. Her test would take around five and a quarter minutes. She intended to give it everything she'd got.

'I don't think I've ever been so proud of you,' said Mrs Smith. 'I mean, to score forty-eight point five and lie ninth in a field of fifty-eight horses is a tremendous achievement by any standard. To do it after that moronic boy had filled your head with nonsense about Peter is simply extraordinary. I have to say that your half-pass left was one of the best I've ever seen. I'd have given you a ten.'

Casey grinned. 'Thanks. I was still pretty happy with a nine. In a strange way, what Scott said motivated me to try even harder. At least, it did after I realised that if Peter's helping the police it must be because he cares what happens to Dad. All of a sudden, I felt as if I had everyone I love most on my side. It helped. You can't believe how much.'

It was only when the door to Casey's hotel room had closed that her teacher allowed herself to collapse against the wall with a groan. She massaged her abdomen with one hand. Perhaps it had to do with the tension of the day, but the pain this evening was close to unbearable. Getting through dinner without letting Casey see how much she was suffering was the hardest thing she'd ever done.

With effort, she limped the short distance along the corridor to her own room. When she opened the door, an envelope slid across the carpet. She picked it up. It was addressed to her, not Casey. As with the original note, the words were cut from a magazine and glued onto the page.

When she'd finished reading it, she sat down before she fell down. The combination of pain and shock were too great for her. The letter quivered in her hand. Finally she found the strength to put it in the safe. She wanted more than anything to put a match to it, but she was wise enough to know that it was likely to be required as evidence.

She picked up the phone. The threat in the letter was directed at her pupil, but it laid the responsibility for Casey's safety squarely on the shoulders of Angelica Smith. If Casey and Storm were not among the leaders at the end of cross-country day, they'd meet with great harm.

The voice of the hotel operator burst into the room and made her jump. 'Good evening. How may I direct your call?'

Mrs Smith hesitated. If she made the wrong decision,

Casey might pay with her life. Then again, doing nothing was no longer an option. Long experience had taught her that in times of great danger, instinct could be a formidable weapon. It was her gut that she listened to now.

'Good evening, operator. Would you be kind enough to put me through to the Metropolitan Police in London, England. I'd like to speak to Detective Inspector Lenny McLeod.'

17

WHEN MCLEOD HUNG up after talking to Angelica Smith, Peter noted that his entire bearing had changed. They were like two great generals coming together and agreeing on a battle plan – a high-risk one, but still a plan.

'How soon can you get hold of your passport?" McLeod demanded.

'What's going on? Where are we going?'

'Casey's life is in danger. We're going to Lexington asap. Now how quickly do you think you can get your hands on your passport?'

Peter felt the rage inside him bubble up again at the thought of anyone harming Casey. Now, more than ever, he was glad that McLeod had agreed to let him assist with the investigation. As painful as it was, it was a great deal better than doing nothing. He checked his watch. 'It's just after five p.m. If I set off as soon as the evening rush hour is over, I could probably make it home by midnight. I could drive back at the crack of dawn and be in London by midday or sooner.'

McLeod shook his head. 'Not good enough. I need you here working with me through the night, and we're going to be taking the first available flight to Lexington tomorrow. I'll send a courier and have him meet us at the airport. We won't make it before Casey rides the cross-country, but I don't share Angelica Smith's concern that the blackmailers – there's more than one, I'm sure of it – will hurt her if she isn't leading after the second day. It doesn't make sense that they would go to all this trouble only to destroy their star performer mid-competition. No, they'll wait till the show jumping phase. Come hell or high water, we have to be there by then. Casey's life may depend on it.'

'What are you going to say to Chief Superintendent Grady?'

'I'm going to tell him what he wants to hear.'

'What's that?'

'That I have some unmentionable illness and am likely to be laid up for quite some time, unable to pursue the investigation.'

'Gout?' Grady practically spat the word into the phone, making no secret of his disgust. 'Is that a real illness? It sounds like something from Victorian times.'

'I'm afraid it's very real indeed. The symptoms are quite unpleasant. I can describe them if you like.'

'Please, spare me the details. This is most unfortunate, McLeod. I was counting on you. How long will you be laid up?'

'It's hard to say, sir. I apologise for letting you down, chief superintendent, especially when you showed such faith in bringing me into the investigation.'

'Say no more about it, McLeod. These things happen. Take as long as you need to recover. Fortunately, the Roland Blue case is ticking along nicely. Any problems, we'll deal with them here. Hope to see you soon.'

'Thanks, sir. Good to know you're keeping on top of things.'

'Oh, I am McLeod, I definitely am.'

McLeod glared up at the departures board at Paddington Station. 'The platform number should be up there by now. Do you think the Heathrow Express has been delayed?'

'If it has and we miss our flight, it'll be your fault,' said Peter. 'I told you we should have left an hour earlier.

I don't understand how you can take so long in the bathroom.'

'And I don't understand why you had to iron all your shirts before you put them in the suitcase. They're only going to get crumpled along the way. Oh this is getting ridiculous. Where is the wretched train?'

After four entire days together, the grizzled detective and young farrier had formed a friendship likely to last for life, but they were so exhausted they tended to bicker like an old married couple.

Most nights they'd averaged three hours' sleep. The previous night, Peter hadn't slept at all. It wasn't that McLeod's sofa wasn't comfortable. Rather surprisingly, both it and the apartment were simple but tasteful, with neutral tones and a homely feel. McLeod's home revealed a man besotted with two things: horses and music. Guitars and CDs were stacked in every available corner. Horse books filled the shelves and there were photographs or posters of horses on every wall.

No, Peter was tired because he and McLeod had spent every available second searching for inconsistencies in Grady's and Don Alexander's lives outside the police force and a more tangible link between the latter and Casey. The difficulty was that until McLeod knew whom he could trust, no one could know that he was investigating a fellow officer, let alone that a civilian was assisting him.

They'd told only one other person about Operation Storm – Ravi Singh, Roland Blue's boss at the Half

Moon Tailor shop. Convinced that his friend and employee was innocent, he was desperate to help in any way he could.

It was McLeod who scored their first breakthrough. While searching for background information on Don Alexander, he chanced upon an article in a New York tabloid revealing that the detective's new mother-in-law had been left destitute by her fraudster husband. Further investigation revealed that Elizabeth Vale-Edwards had continued to live and prosper on her Long Island estate with no visible means of support.

Don himself appeared to have benefited from the association. In the eighteen months since meeting Isabelle at a polo match, he'd acquired a Mercedes sports car, been on numerous luxury holidays and joined a private club in Shoreditch. He'd told colleagues that his new relations were exceptionally generous people. Now it turned out that the Vale-Edwardses did not have the income to be benevolent. The funds were coming from some mysterious source.

More digging revealed that Elizabeth Vale-Edwards was a renowned equestrian judge and currently a member of the ground jury at the Kentucky Three-Day Event.

By then, all sorts of alarm bells were ringing for the investigators. Mrs Smith's phone call confirmed that they were on the right trail.

'Surely, you have enough evidence now to go to someone higher up the chain than Grady?' urged Peter.

'If Casey's life has been threatened, she needs the police to step in today, not on Sunday when it might be too late. You should insist that Mrs Smith stop her from riding in the cross-country.'

But McLeod was adamant that if the blackmail plot was exposed in mid-operation, the risk to Casey could be far greater.

'It would also allow the perpetrators – whoever they are, and we have no proof of anything at this stage – to slip away scot free. We need them to show their hand so that we can catch them in the act if possible. Try not to worry. I've been in touch with a friend of mine in the FBI. He's on the case in the US, and between now and when we leave, you and I will carry on digging in London. We'll find out who's behind this and get to Casey in time.'

'You mean you *hope* we'll get there in time. There are no guarantees.'

'No, there are no guarantees.'

It was as he paced beneath the train departures board for the twentieth time that McLeod became aware of a commotion. A tattooed giant burst from the crowd, shoving people aside. Sweat poured off him.

'Oy, you, copper!' he cried.

'Rick Crawley! What on earth are you doing here?

Fleeing the country or something? Robbed a bank and heading for the Caribbean?'

Big Red was hunched over, gasping for breath. 'Here I am, doing you a favour and you immediately jump to a negative conclusion.'

'Mmm, now why would I do that? How could I possibly think badly of a man with a string of convictions for theft, fraud and assault. Peter, meet Rick Crawley, one of our most upstanding citizens. What favour are you wanting to do me, Mr Crawley?'

'Here, you could ruin my reputation with talk like that. Don't listen to him, kid. It's a pack of lies. Not that you deserve it, detective, but I have something that might interest you. I was planning to leave it with old Ravi at the Half Moon Tailor shop. Let me tell you, it's not in my interests to be seen consorting with the law.'

The platform number flashed up on the departures board. McLeod grabbed his suitcase. 'Make it quick, Crawley. We have a plane to catch.'

'Anyhow, Ravi was adamant that I give it to you myself. Said it could be a matter of life and death. Said that you and Casey's boyfriend, which I'm guessing is you, kid, were flying out the country practically within the hour on some kind of mercy mission, but that I might still catch you.'

'We have four minutes to make it to the train,' said Peter in agitation.

'All right, all right,' grumbled Crawley. Reaching into his suit pocket, he fished out a USB stick.

McLeod took it from him. 'Is this what I think it is?'

Crawley used a handkerchief to mop the sweat from his brow. 'See, what happened is this. After Roland was banged up in jail his daughter came to see me. Full of accusations, like yourself. I was angry at first, but I admired her spirit. I got to thinking about her father. He's a good sort. Genuine. Not a bad bone in his body. Not really. No way he would have been involved in that art warehouse caper. That was a bad business, that. Very bad. I got to thinking that he must have been stitched up.'

'Get to the point,' barked McLeod.

'Then I read in the paper that the CCTV video that might have proved his innocence has taken a walk. I had a little chat to a mate who lives in Redwing Tower. For reasons of personal security, he has his own cameras installed around the place. We watched it back and it showed Roland going back to his flat after leaving Ravi clear as day. Doesn't open the front door till next morning.'

He winked slyly at McLeod. 'So you'll have to release him, won't you? Can't keep him locked up when he's plainly innocent. And don't forget, copper, you owe me now. You and Casey's old man.'

McLeod sighed. 'Allow me to explain something, Crawley. You are a criminal and I am an officer of the law. That means that I don't owe you anything apart from justice and nor does Casey's dad, who has been

163

put in this position through no fault of his own. You, on the other hand, owe society a great deal. That doesn't mean I'm not grateful to you for your help. What you've done is an incredible thing. I shall never forget this. But my advice to you would be to think of it as good karma. By doing an honourable thing, you've taken one small step towards making up for past wrongs and helping the universe to become a better place.'

Crawley moaned a little longer, purely for effect, but he was rather taken with the notion that, for once, he'd made a positive contribution to the world. However, he made it clear to McLeod that he'd hunt him down and crush him like a bug if he did not 'do right by old Roland and his horse girl'.

He offered Peter his usual bone-crushing handshake and was startled when the boy looked him in the eye and crushed his hand right back. Peter spent his days hanging onto the hooves of boisterous eventers and temperamental thoroughbred stallions. Rick Crawley's grip was nothing compared to those.

The giant studied him with renewed respect. 'When you see your girl in Kentucky, wish her luck from Big Red.'

At the words 'your girl', Peter's stomach twisted into a hard knot. He'd already resolved to leave Kentucky the second he knew Casey was safe. 'I'd be glad to. Thanks for what you've done. You might have changed everything.'

As Big Red walked away, his brawny figure towering over the holiday crowds, McLeod shook his head.

'Rick Crawley. Of all the unlikely heroes ... Who says there's no such thing as redemption?'

18

FOR MUCH OF its three-decade history, the
Kentucky Three-Day Event had been sensibly held
in late April, the week before Badminton, when the
azaleas and rhododendrons are in full bloom and the
temperature is close to perfect for eventing. In this
particular year, however, rival television networks had
clashed over the timing. Ultimately, the organisers had
no choice but to move the championship to the end of
May when temperatures soared in America's southern
states. As a result, cross-country day in Lexington was
so sizzling that by 11 a.m. you could have fried an egg on
the bonnet of any car in the park.

Casey's start time was at 2.50 p.m. By mid-afternoon
the first-aid tent was seeing a steady stream of visitors

suffering from dehydration and sunstroke, and several of the European horses, unused to the humidity, had wilted on the cross-country. They'd finished well over the optimum time of eleven minutes and eleven seconds.

It was here, though, that Ethan's boot camp training for Casey, and Mrs Smith's dedication to alternative therapies and achieving maximum fitness for Storm had paid off. After a morning in which he'd had a relaxing dawn stroll across the park, been massaged, read to and had his legs soothed with an aloe vera paste, Storm was as cool as a cucumber. Casey, too, felt sharp and alert. She was buzzing with nerves and adrenalin, but she was focused. She had blocked any thought of the blackmailer from her head. If she was going to achieve the clear round she needed, she could think of nothing else but the next fence, the next stride.

The cross-country course had been open for competitors to view for several days now and on Thursday, she and Mrs Smith had walked and measured it until they knew every blade of grass.

'You have to be so familiar with it that if you were parachuted into it at midnight, blindfold, you'd know where you were,' said her teacher. 'There are twenty-eight obstacles over four miles. A split second of hesitation or a moment of indecision at any one of them could result in a run-out, a refusal or a fall. Equally, if you choose the short route at, say, the final water, and have a disaster, when playing it safe and risking a few time penalties would have resulted in a clear, you'd kick yourself.

'Remember that you are Storm's eyes. He will be going out onto the course blind. His ability to get round in the optimum time safely and with no faults entirely rests on your ability to communicate to him what lies ahead. And, as you can see, what lies ahead is full of trickery.'

Casey did see and it was the thought uppermost in her mind as she and Storm waited to start. William Fox-Pitt, a past winner, had warned that Derek di Grazia's course designs were deceptively simple. He had a particular genius for playing with terrain to make nerve-janglingly hard jumps look like something a novice could breeze over. An ill-prepared rider would not be aware that he or she had been fooled until it was too late.

'That's why it's crucial that you don't get ahead of yourself,' Mrs Smith had said as Casey had left the warm-up area. 'Give Storm a good look at every fence. Ride safely. I'll be with you on every stride.'

Casey grinned. 'Like an angel on my shoulder.'

'Like an angel on your shoulder.'

Storm burst forward. Casey had a blurred view of trees, colourful picnickers and a skein of wild geese, crying overhead, then the first fence flew beneath them and they were on their way, riding for her father's life.

She knew nothing of the blackmailer's vicious letter to Mrs Smith the previous night, nor had her teacher said anything about her phone conversation with McLeod. The detective had been adamant that Casey must know nothing that might distract her or in any way give her enemies a clue that they might be on the verge of being discovered.

He had given Mrs Smith an emergency FBI number to call if anyone attempted to approach her, but few details about how the investigation was progressing. 'Fear not,' he'd told her. 'The cavalry is on its way and should be in Lexington by ten on Saturday evening.'

Until then there were FBI 'watchers' in the crowd who would step in to protect Casey should that become necessary.

Oblivious to any of this, Casey urged Storm strongly down the slope to fence five, the first tough question on the course. Mrs Smith had cautioned her that the problem with this particular obstacle would not be leaping the log into the water. It would be the wall of sound that came from the crowds. 'For Storm, who'll be emerging from the trees and relative quiet of the early fences, it'll be extremely intimidating. Keep your finger on the button.'

Casey did as she'd instructed, driving Storm forward while reassuring him with her voice. Into the water they went, spray flying up around them. Storm took three strides over the log and brush and another four to the Goose at the top of the rise. Then they were out and galloping. Storm's ears were pricked and there was joy in his long stride. He was, Casey could tell, in his element.

As he soared over the sixth, Tobacco Stripping Bench, the stresses of the past month fell from Casey's shoulders. She forgot everything except that this was what she lived for – these glorious moments. Storm's happiness was infectious too, and they were as one as they took the trakehner and turned sharply left for the Brush Water Challenge.

Storm seemed to fall for ever, plummeting into the lake below with tremendous force. It took all Casey's skill and balance to hold her position and line before the cabin at the top of the slope was upon them. After that, it was a relief to have three breather fences in a row. She even smiled as they negotiated the twelfth, which featured a large wooden squirrel gnawing a fallen tree.

Only weeks earlier Storm, with his racehorse instincts and love of speed, would have landed on the downslope of the Sheep Shelter thirteenth and accelerated, totally out of control. Now he landed fast, but Casey was able to check him before he took over. She turned him tightly and allowed him to have a good look before lining him up for the Double Corners. Storm made it look easy and before she knew it they were round the loop and heading for home.

The heat rolled over them in waves, making a mirage of the nineteenth obstacle, the water complex. The previous night Casey had barely slept a wink. One after another, worries had piled up on her. Lying in bed, she'd lifted her phone at least a dozen times to text Peter, but had deleted them every time. She longed to hear his voice. Why had she never told him she loved him? How could she have let things get so bad between them?

Mostly though, she'd worried about the cross-country. She was terrified that she'd fail her father, or that the blackmailer would renege on their one-sided deal. Her biggest fear was that he'd hurt her and Storm when they were most vulnerable – out on the cross-country course. Over and over, she pictured the man with the nightmare face. In the absence of any other suspects, she remained certain that he was her tormenter.

Meditation and a dawn hack had helped to banish those images, but in the simmering heat the lack of sleep caught up with her. Dizzy, she swayed in the saddle as Storm soared over the post and rails and plunged into the water. He blasted through, popping neatly over the two wooden ducks and bounding out to huge applause. Storm's silver coat was dark with foam and water, but he was breathing more easily than he had been at this stage at Badminton.

As he breezed through the Normandy Bank, Casey began to feel almost euphoric. They were only seven obstacles from home.

The Keeper's Brush was big but straightforward and fences twenty-four and twenty-five required accuracy rather than nerve. She forced herself to concentrate hard on the approach. It was here that Allison Springer, pathfinding in 2011 after a sublime dressage on her thoroughbred, Arthur, had had a fall and been eliminated.

'It's not over till it's over,' Mrs Smith had warned her. 'One missed stride and the easiest fence in the world can be devastating.'

The last real challenge was the offset brushes. Casey's watch beeped. She was slightly ahead of time. Taking her teacher's advice, she went the long route, counting on Storm's explosive speed to help them avoid time penalties. The penultimate fence, an arch, flashed beneath them. 'Go on, Storm!' cried Casey.

They rocketed towards the final hurdle, Produce Table. The crowd, with their upturned, smiling faces, formed a rainbow corridor for her. One fence lay between her and a clear round. One fence ...

A yapping dog darted from beneath the ropes. Storm swerved violently. Later, Casey would credit Ethan's tortuous Swiss ball balance exercises for saving her, for although she lurched from the saddle and grabbed a handful of mane, she didn't fall.

Enraged, Storm bolted towards the Produce Table, taking off over the fruit and flowers before Casey had recovered her seat. She had to use all her strength to cling on. It was as he started to come down that he caught the edge of the table with a foot.

Casey had the sinking feeling that precedes a bad fall, coupled with the sensation that time has slowed to a crawl. She saw the shocked face of a small girl, mouth agape as she stared up at the soaring horse. She heard the dog barking madly and the far-away drone of an aeroplane.

Then, on the periphery of her vision, she had a rapid, sketchy impression of the man who'd attacked her at White Oaks. It was something about the way he moved.

The thought flashed through her head that he'd planned all along to kill them. That he hadn't succeeded then and he was going to do it now.

She braced herself for the impact. It didn't happen. With cat-like athleticism, Storm righted himself. He twisted in mid-air and landed awkwardly, but was bounding forward almost instantly. Somehow Casey stayed on.

Risking a glance over her shoulder, she spotted the man straight away. He didn't have a nightmare face at all. He was handsome in a well-groomed way and wearing black trousers and a blue polo shirt. He had a phone to his ear and was already walking away. She'd been mistaken. She'd survived and there was still everything to play for.

Storm was tired, but not so tired that he couldn't produce a final, blistering surge of speed. When they crossed the line four seconds inside the optimum time, he pulled up only reluctantly. Sweat was pouring from his silver flanks, but he looked so pleased with himself it was almost comical.

'You,' Casey told him as she slid from the saddle and hugged first him and then her teacher, 'are a wonder horse. Don't you agree, Mrs Smith?'

She laughed. 'I agree that he's a superstar but not that

he should have all the credit. Casey, that was a cross-country masterclass. If it hadn't been for that imbecile of a dog owner, you'd have had a near flawless round. Riding-wise, I couldn't fault it.'

To Casey's astonishment, her teacher, usually so cool and composed, burst into tears. 'Oh, my dear, thank goodness you're safe.'

'Of course I'm safe,' said Casey, hugging her again. 'Storm took care of me like he always does.'

But she knew that Mrs Smith knew how close they'd come to disaster. Another millimetre and they'd have had the most feared accident in eventing and the cause of almost all deaths – a rotational fall.

Those were the falls where the horse effectively did a cartwheel, often landing on the rider and killing them. Air jackets that inflated on impact had made an enormous difference, but they were not failsafe.

She lowered her voice. 'Mrs Smith, it's almost over. I'm another step closer to freeing Dad. We just have to pray that our letter-writing friend does the right thing. If he reneges on his promise, I don't know what we're going to do.'

Before her coach could answer, Casey was engulfed by journalists. They all wanted to know one thing: could the youngest Badminton champion in history do the double in Kentucky on her one-dollar horse?

'I wouldn't like to say. Show jumping is not Storm's strong suit.' Glancing up at the leaderboard, on which she was lying fourth, she grinned cheekily. 'But if I were

Jock Padget, Jenny Elverson or Blake Tetherington, I'd be looking in my rear-view mirror tomorrow.'

In the shade of a sycamore tree, the man in the blue polo shirt was on his phone. His voice was jubilant. 'Did you see that, Lizzie? We couldn't have scripted it better – although I must admit I almost had a coronary when the horse left a leg behind at the last. The girl's among the leaders, exactly as we planned. Now are you going to break the news to her that she has to lose tomorrow, or shall I?

19

AT 4.02 A.M., at the exact moment that Lenny McLeod and Peter were checking out of a soulless beige Chicago hotel, having missed their Lexington connection and failing to get on an alternative flight, the phone rang in Casey's hotel room.

She dragged herself out of a nightmare in which she was being pursued on Storm by a headless horseman and fumbled for the phone. 'H'llo.'

'Good morning, Casey Blue!' a woman said brightly. 'This is your wake-up call.'

Casey flicked on the lamp and squinted at her watch. Her brain clicked slowly into gear. It was Sunday, the day of the show jumping. She'd hoped to have a lie-in to give her body and mind the best possible chance to bounce back from the onslaught of the cross-country. Mrs Smith had been under strict instructions to leave her in peace.

'I didn't order a wake-up call.'

Then, as a feeling of dread came over her: 'Who is this?'

'Would you believe me if I said a friend? No, I didn't think so. Don't hang up. That would be a mistake. And silly besides. If you do what we say, you have nothing to fear from us. You're a very necessary part of our operation, Casey. We need you to finish the task that we've set for you. Added to which, we're delighted with your progress. You and your knacker's yard horse have excelled yourselves.'

'You're sick,' Casey almost shouted into the phone. 'You're psychotic. You're destroying my dad's life – and mine, for that matter. You're also a coward. Why don't you show yourself and we can talk about this face to face?'

The caller was silent. Casey slumped against the headboard. If this hellish experience was ever over, she was going to persuade an honest detective, if such a person existed, to hunt those responsible to the ends of the earth. She had to listen for voice clues. If the call couldn't be traced, she needed to be able to identify the woman by her accent or speech pattern or inflexions in her voice.

That was perhaps the biggest shock – that at least one of her tormenters was a woman.

'If I'm doing so wonderfully, why are you calling to terrorise me at the crack of dawn? Frightening me out of my wits and making me lose sleep is not going to improve my performance, you know,' she prompted.

'That's precisely why I'm calling. The goalposts have been moved, you see. You are no longer required to win. Instead we need you to lose.'

'You're joking.'

'Afraid not.'

Casey was so incensed she almost dropped the phone. 'Are you out of your mind? Have you any concept of how hard I've had to work to get into this position? I've nearly killed myself. You and your partners in crime almost killed me with that stunt you pulled at White Oaks. I've pushed my horse to his limits. And now you're telling me that it's all been for nothing. That I could have lounged around in front of the TV for the past month and come here and lost, because that's what you wanted all along?'

'Keep your voice down or I'll hang up,' the woman warned. 'Don't you understand what this is about yet? Haven't you figured it out? Don't worry. At the end of the day, everybody gets what they want. We'll get our hands on a lot of cash and you'll get the CCTV footage proving your father is innocent.'

Her laugh was chilly, sending an odd shiver through Casey. 'Before I go, are we clear on what you need to do this afternoon in the show jumping? In the unlikely event that you and Storm Warning look on course to win the title, you must throw the last fence.'

'No.'

'No?'

'No,' said Casey. 'I'm not going to do that. Why should I? What if you move the goalposts again? What if I have a chance to win and deliberately blow it by knocking down the last fence, and you refuse to give me the tape. I'll have lost everything. My dad will still be in jail and I'll have missed out on the chance to become the youngest rider in history to win both Badminton and Kentucky, something he desperately wants for me.'

'You have no choice but to trust us to deliver the tape after you've lost,' the woman said coldly. 'If you double-cross us, your father will spend his life behind bars. But I don't believe you'll make that decision. You're not the sort of girl who'd choose winning over love.'

'You don't know me,' Casey said obstinately. 'I might.'

'Do that and we'll take steps to ensure that losing is your only option.'

20

THE STABLES WERE almost deserted and dawn a peach blush in the sky when Casey unlatched the yard gate on Sunday morning. She wore an old pair of chocolate-coloured breeches that she'd brought as a spare and her favourite grey T-shirt with the sleeves cut off. Storm was so thrilled to see her that he almost kicked the door down before she could open it.

Casey put her forehead to his and breathed in his heavenly smell. When her father was arrested she'd temporarily forgotten that if life got on top of her, Storm was her place of sanctuary. Mrs Smith's wise words had helped her remember. 'The horse is always there,' she'd said. 'They're always waiting.'

Running her hands over Storm's hocks, Casey was relieved to see that there was no swelling or tenderness after the cross-country. He'd never had any problems with inflammation before but you never knew. After the dog incident at the last obstacle, he'd hit the ground hard. It would be ironic if, after everything they'd been through, Storm failed to get through the trot-up that preceded the show jumping.

After running a quick dandy brush over him and giving him a handful of pony nuts, she put a headcollar on him and led him out to the mounting block. When she swung onto his bare back, he felt warm and solid beneath her.

'Got a death wish?' asked a sleepy-eyed groom as he passed. 'If he spooks while you're out in the park, it'll be off to the races with you. He looks as if he has some go in him.'

Casey waved the end of the lead rope at him and continued through the gate. 'He does have some go in him,' she said over her shoulder, 'but that's all right with me. Storm and I, we love to race the wind.'

It was true that she didn't have a death wish. Quite the opposite. As soon as she'd hung up the phone that morning, she'd paused only to have a lightning shower and brush her teeth before catching the hotel shuttle to the Kentucky Horse Park, a five-minute journey. Her best chance of surviving the day ahead and outwitting her enemies was to get as close to Storm as possible. She needed him on her side and in tune with her.

In a way, the blackmailers had made life easy for her. She'd been worried about Storm's show jumping from the start. Now if she had a fence down, it wouldn't be the end of the world. She'd get the tape and her father would be free. So why did the thought of deliberately losing make her feel so gutted?

It was not that she was mourning her lost chance at history, the title, and the Grand Slam. Without love, the greatest prizes on earth were empty – nothing more than names in record books and bits of silverware gathering dust on shelves. It was the love of friends and family that made the celebration of those things special. It was love that made them mean something.

No, she was enraged that these strangers thought they could manipulate her like a puppet on a string.

Casey and Storm loved to win, *lived* to win, and Badminton had shown them that with hard work and the right training they might be able to do it a lot. Now they were being ordered to do something that went against their very nature.

She could have done what the blackmailers wanted as long as it meant winning to save her father. There was honour in that. It injured nobody. If she was now expected to do something illegal, unethical and dishonourable, something that went against the core of her being, it was – to use an American expression – a game-changer.

Storm stretched out across the park, his walk relaxed and easy. The sun was a red ball climbing lazily above

182

the statue of Man O'War, the legendary racehorse. Casey felt her spirits lift. It was hard to be depressed in the face of the birds' joyous chorus. When she and Storm reached the trail to the lake, a palomino came to the paddock fence to greet them, leaving emerald hoofprints in the carpet of dew.

Casey knew she was taking a risk riding Storm bareback and in only a headcollar, but to her it was worth it. She wanted to remind him of their work at White Oaks and the beach at Camber Sands. His free spirit was their greatest weapon.

Back home, some of the riding centre instructors had been frank in their criticism of Mrs Smith's methods. Morag said that in twenty-three years of teaching, she'd never met anyone who thought that preparing a horse for one of the world's biggest championships using only a neck rope was a good idea.

'Anyone would think that you were determined to take last place,' she'd said snippily to Casey 'I can't understand what the pair of you are playing at. You won at Badminton using one method. Now you want to change it in three weeks using a rope, as if he was a seaside donkey. It's bonkers, no other way of looking at it.'

In fact, the rope was only used on the beach and during warm-ups and cool-downs. The rest of the time Storm worked in a double bridle or the bridle and drop noseband he used in the cross-country. Mrs Smith's aim was to unite horse and rider and refine the aids.

'If you aid subtly, the horse will learn to respond subtly. Practise half halts at all gaits and all tempos and you'll teach Storm the balance and collection you see in the best dressage horses.'

At first, Casey had been frustrated that they didn't spend more time on Storm's show jumping, but her teacher had convinced her that if she got the foundation right, everything else would follow.

'For the horse, there are two keys to success in all disciplines,' she said. 'Positive body tension coupled with a looseness and suppleness of gait. Combine them and you're halfway there.'

Casey guided Storm down to the water. The problem was that whether she decided to give in to the blackmailers' demand and lose, or defy them and attempt to win, she needed to be more than halfway there. She needed the extra fifty per cent.

The idea of how to find it had come to her as she lay fuming in bed after hanging up the phone. Now that she was here it seemed both eccentric and ill-advised, especially with the trot-up less than three hours away, but in her mind she was already committed.

The rising sun had turned the lake a vibrant hue of rose. It curled away in butterfly ripples as she guided Storm in. He stepped delicately in among the water lilies. At first he was confused and jogged a few strides, eyes on stalks as the ducks scattered, expecting to be asked to jump something. When he found she just wanted him to relax and enjoy himself, he settled down instantly.

Casey had never swum on a horse and she doubted Storm had ever been in deep water himself. On the beach at Camber Sands, they'd galloped along the lacy fringes of the waves, but gone in no further. But here, as she'd expected, the bottom of the lake shelved sharply.

As the ground disappeared beneath him, he plunged forward snorting. Casey felt a momentary rush of panic. What if this was a colossal mistake? Storm's back sank beneath her and cold water swilled around her kidneys, making her gasp.

Then, quite suddenly, he was swimming. Except that it felt as if they were floating. As if they were no longer earthbound mortals, constrained by earthly troubles, but creatures of myth and joy and light. A girl and a silver unicorn, or even a centaur – half-girl and half-horse.

The rose-gold water parted before them. Casey laughed with the sheer exhilaration of it. Storm swam boldly towards the shore and then, like a child reluctant to leave the fun of the pool, he did a second circuit.

They came flying out of the water at a full gallop, pink spray flying up all around them. Casey, with nothing but a rope and her leg aids to control Storm, wasn't worried in the least. She knew that she'd been right to bring him here. Together, they'd found something without which the best tack in the world and ten years of schooling was worthless. They'd connected in mind, body and spirit.

They were joined.

21

'SIR, YOU NEED to calm down,' said the woman at the airline check-in desk, who was wearing so much mascara that her eyelids blinked as sleepily as an iguana's under the weight of it.

'But you promised!' ranted McLeod. 'I told you it was a life and death matter and you gave me your word that you'd get us on the first available plane out of Chicago this morning.'

'Sir, if you raise your voice to me once more, I, personally, will see to it that you go nowhere at all.'

'I'm sorry. Truly, I apologise. I've had no sleep. However, you can't blame me for getting upset. The only thing that stopped us driving the seven hours from Chicago to Lexington last night was your solemn promise that you'd get us on a 5.30 a.m. flight, which you admit you forgot to do. Now you inform us that we're on the 9.30 a.m. flight, which is delayed for at least an hour for technical reasons.'

'And that's my fault why exactly?' She glared defiantly at the other people in the queue. 'What do ya'll expect me to do about it? You want me to go out onto the runway and fix it myself?'

'Of course we don't,' Peter said. He smiled in an attempt to placate her. 'We appreciate that you're doing your best under difficult circumstances.'

Steering McLeod away, he bought a couple of coffees and bagels with cream cheese and carried them to an area of vacant seats.

'It'll be okay, Lenny,' he soothed, although increasingly he had the feeling that okay was the very last thing it was going to be. He'd forgotten his charger and his mobile had died. Now if Casey called or texted, he'd never know.

McLeod gulped down a mouthful of black coffee. He consulted the sports pages of the local paper. 'According to this, Casey's start time in the show jumping is at 2.52 p.m. Provided the flight delay is only an hour, we'll be in Lexington by midday. Even allowing for traffic, we should be at the Kentucky Horse Park within the hour. Plenty of time to get our bearings and stake out the arena.

'You're right. Everything's going to be fine.'

Over the years, Angelica Smith had consistently refused to own a mobile phone, for the simple reason that she'd never felt the need for one. Until now. Now she decided she was the most bird-brained dinosaur that ever lived.

If she'd had a mobile and had thought to take Detective McLeod's number, she'd be able to tell him about Casey's early-morning call and how the game had changed and Casey and Storm were now supposed to lose. She could have rung Peter and begged him to call Casey and plead with her not to continue.

She might also have some idea when this supposed cavalry was going to arrive and what form it might take, instead of glowering suspiciously at everyone in the vicinity.

Grooms and riders she'd known for years now looked sinister to her, and she couldn't decide whether the woman with the brown bob and dark glasses, who was leaning against the paddock fence reading a programme upside down, was an FBI agent or the blackmailer in disguise.

When a golden-haired man rather arrogantly enquired about Casey's chances, she'd nearly snapped his head off. 'She's one of the best young riders out there. Of course she has a shot at the title.'

Never had she felt so sick or scared on her pupil's behalf, and her nerves only worsened when she arrived at the collecting ring to find Storm rolling a pole. Stifling her despair, she stepped forward with what she hoped was a confident smile.

'Don't let it worry you. Trust in the preparation you've done to see you through. This close to show time you should be concentrating on only two things. You want Storm to be making a good shape over the fences and to be responsive and rideable between jumps. Trot him in circles and do some leg yielding to get him stretching and thinking. Good. Now take him over the cross pole and onto the upright. Keep your leg on and your hands soft and aim for a deep take-off point.'

After Casey had cleared both without mishap, Mrs Smith raised the height of the cross pole and changed the vertical into an oxer. Thanks to an early morning session with a local Chinese acupuncturist, her pain had completely gone. She felt alert and vital, ready to cope with almost anything.

But she had no idea what form that anything would take. She'd tried everything in her power to persuade Casey to withdraw from the show jumping. 'I'm counselling you not to do this. It's not worth it. There is nothing to say that these wicked people will honour their part of the bargain.'

But despite what must have been a traumatic phone call, Casey had radiated determination. 'I'm not withdrawing. I've come this far. I'm going to finish this thing. I refuse to let them break me.'

'Does that mean you're going to do what they're

asking and deliberately knock down a pole or cause a refusal if it looks as if you're about to win? Or are you going for the title?'

'Don't know. I'm going to see how I feel when I'm in the arena.'

She'd cantered away before Mrs Smith could grab Storm's bridle and demand again that she withdraw.

In truth, Casey's earlier calm had been rattled. After breakfast, she'd finally given in and sent Peter a text. At first she'd written, *I've heard what you're doing for my father. Thank you so much. It means everything to me. Love Casey x*

Following much deliberation she'd erased it and put simply: *Wish you were here x*

Nearly six hours later, there was still no reply.

Now, just minutes before the most important round of her life, she was once again obsessing over Peter. Maybe Scott had got it all wrong. If Peter really were helping Detective McLeod, surely he'd have let her know? If he retained the smallest vestige of feelings for her, surely he'd have replied to her text, if only to wish her luck?

The steward signalled.

Mrs Smith came over to her. 'Casey, you need to go right this second.'

Casey's mobile beeped. She hesitated.

'Hand that to me and go. Focus. Think fluidity, patience, lightness and clarity of aids.'

Casey tossed her the phone and trotted out of the gate, all her thoughts now on the challenge ahead. There'd been eleven clear rounds. Storm was tired, but he was willing to do this for her. That was his way of returning her love. He'd invested his heart and soul into pleasing her on the cross-country. He'd potentially saved their lives on the last fence. He deserved better than to be forced to lose.

So first, they would show the crowd what he was made of. They would set the place on fire. Then, and only then, would they submit to the blackmailer's demand.

A man stepped into her path. In the Kentucky sunlight, he looked pale and dishevelled and yet he had presence that the most expensively groomed heads of business and state in the white marquees lining the stadium could not hope to have matched.

'Get back!' commanded the steward. 'Out of the way!'

'I'm afraid I can't. I'm a British police officer and I have an urgent message for this young lady.'

A frisson of excitement rippled through the officials, grooms and riders within earshot.

Casey was in shock. 'Detective Inspector McLeod! What are you doing here?'

'No time to explain. All you need to know is that we have the evidence we need and your father will be freed within hours. Now go and show them what you're made of, Casey Blue. By the way, Peter is with me and he says good luck.'

22

C ASEY CANTERED INTO the stadium with the detective's words running through her head like a river of flame. *Your father will be freed within hours ...*

It was beyond her comprehension how this could have come about – Peter and this detective, both in Kentucky and seemingly responsible for foiling the blackmailers. Miraculous seemed too ordinary a term for it.

But there was no time to think about it now. She had a job to do. For reasons unknown, she'd been handed a gift and she had ninety-two seconds to make the most of it. Thirteen obstacles, which equated to sixteen jumping efforts, stood between her and the title. All she and Storm had to do was clear them in the optimum time.

The conditions were close to perfect. Overhead,

milkshake clouds frothed and bubbled. Underfoot, the synthetic surface was cushioned but firmly supportive. A breeze took the sting out of the heat. Its musical whisper was the only sound in the tense stadium.

As Casey and Storm cleared the oxer, the crowd leaned forward as one. The leading riders had still to go, but it was this girl and her one-dollar horse who'd captured their imagination. Storm Warning flowed like mercury from one brightly coloured fence to another.

Earlier, Casey and Mrs Smith had watched Clayton Fredericks, Oliver Townend, Sinead Halpin and Fraser Goff jump, trying to learn from the lines they chose, the corners they cut and the strides they did or didn't take. Fraser clocked up twenty-four faults on his dapple-grey, Reckless Lad, a famously tidy cross-country horse, but one who on that occasion seemed blithely unconcerned about kicking show jumps from their cups.

Casey had sympathised with Fraser. After the frightening solidity of the cross-country phase, the show jumps seemed feather-light. The merest brush sent them floating off into space. Casey had had visions of Storm clocking up some kind of record for the most show jumping faults ever recorded.

But that wasn't how she was thinking now. Ethan had taught her that sportsmen who talked about 'trying' to win were half-expecting to fail. She had to believe with every fibre of her being that if she rode well enough and her tactics were good enough, victory was hers for the taking.

And with her father safe and soon to be free, winning was about much more than the title. It was about standing up to the blackmailers, valiant and uncowed. It was about remembering she and Storm were one – a centaur. It was about the truth.

Each obstacle honoured a famous equestrian farm or landmark in Kentucky. Casey let the reins slip through her hands as Storm gave a huge leap over the Keeneland Race Course jump, the Root and Riddle Equine Hospital jump, the iconic red and white barn of Calumet Farm, and the green and gold triple. He felt invincible beneath her. There was a brazen confidence in the way he soared over the twelfth fence, a Mississippi paddle steamer heading up a cobalt blue water trough.

As they turned to the last, its standards modelled on the twin spires of Churchill Downs racetrack, home of the Kentucky Derby, Casey remembered the caller's threat. *In the unlikely event that you and Storm Warning look on course to have a clear round and a shot at the title, you must throw the last fence ... or we'll take steps to ensure that losing is your only option ...*

Her father was free. What was the worst they could do to her?

Determinedly, she rode Storm at the fence. His quarters bunched. There was a blinding flash of light. Storm wheeled and screamed. Casey fell in slow motion. She was conscious of the collective shock of an audience of thousands. Pain shot through her shoulder and everything went dark.

'Casey? Casey, can you hear me?'

Casey opened her eyes. Peter and Storm were gazing down at her and it was hard to tell who looked more concerned. She smiled dazedly. 'We really must stop meeting like this.'

McLeod leaned over her. 'Why, is this a regular occurrence?'

'Long story,' Casey told him. 'Now will somebody help me up? We need to call the police.'

'I *am* the police.'

'So you are. Well, in that case you need to find the person or people responsible for—'

But she got no further because Mrs Smith arrived, followed by the paramedics with a stretcher and a couple of officials and everyone seemed to be talking at once. And in the midst of it, like some faraway radio broadcast, the announcer said, 'Casey Blue, riding Storm Warning, has been eliminated for a fall.'

The blackmailer had won.

23

A STORM WAS BREWING, and not just in the heavens. An unprecedented situation had occurred. The last two riders had jumped and Blake Tetherington, the pre-championship favourite, had been judged to have won the Kentucky Three-Day Event with a double clear. But following an appeal lodged by Mrs Smith and McLeod, his crown was being withheld pending an enquiry into the cause of Casey's fall.

'Why is Casey expecting special treatment?' demanded Annabel, the groom from the plane. 'I mean, she's still a kid. She's come here, she's performed out of her skin for most of the three days and then she's had a refusal and taken a tumble. It happens. Get over it.'

'It's not about that, Annie,' said her employer

Jenny Elverson, whose mount, Evergreen Rocket, had inexplicably landed in the water jump, costing her the championship. 'Casey is certain that she saw a flash as Storm was about to take off. She's convinced the jump was sabotaged.'

'Of course she saw a flash; there were about seventeen thousand people taking photos. It's about time Casey Blue learned that the whole world doesn't revolve around her. So what if she's won Badminton? It doesn't mean that they should rewrite the rule book for her.'

'She's not asking to have the rule book rewritten,' said Jenny, losing patience. 'She's asking for fairness and it so happens that I and most of the other riders are on her side. When you watch the replay, there does seem to be a bright flare in the centre of the jump as they approach. Plus that rather attractive British detective who turned up out of nowhere claims to have found powdered glass beneath the jump. Evidence, apparently, that a flash bulb could have been used.'

'If you say so,' Annabel muttered dismissively. 'Personally, I prefer the Welsh farrier who helped Casey up. Did you see his arm muscles? I've made enquiries and have it on good authority that he's single.'

It was Elizabeth Vale-Edwards, chairman of the ground jury, who announced that the judges had considered

Casey Blue's claim of sabotage and found that there was not enough evidence to support it. In her time, Elizabeth had had to put on many Oscar-worthy performances, particularly when dealing with friends whom her late husband had cheated out of money, but now she excelled herself.

With just the right mix of pathos and impartiality, she told the assembled riders, officials and members of the press that the fragments of glass discovered beneath the jump, were so powdery and minuscule that without clear forensic evidence to the contrary they could have come from anywhere. They could have dropped from the pocket of a rider walking the course, or even a carpenter or groundsman days earlier. Equally, the flash visible on the replay could simply be a reflection or glint of sunlight.

'The point,' Elizabeth continued, 'is that twenty-seven other competitors completed the course without incident this afternoon, and eleven of those riders achieved clear rounds. For that reason, we are unanimous in upholding the elimination of Casey Blue, who I'm told is currently with the veterinarian examining her horse, Storm Warning. We wish them both well. Without further ado, I would like to congratulate Blake Teth—'

'I'm sure you would.' McLeod's voice cut clearly through the angry hum that greeted this announcement. 'You would like nothing more than to wipe Casey from the picture and crown Blake as champion so that you can collect your winnings.'

Elizabeth didn't react. 'I have no idea what you're talking about, sir. If you have an official complaint, you're welcome to write a letter—'

'I do have an official complaint,' said McLeod, 'and there are plenty of reporters here to witness it. For the record, I'd like to say that I have a very strong objection to equestrian judges who abuse their position by blackmailing vulnerable young riders ...'

There was a gasp from the gathered scribes and riders.

'... and, when they don't cooperate, resorting to sabotage.'

Elizabeth shot him a look of pure loathing, but she maintained an icy façade. 'I don't know how they do things in your country, but here in the US when we are defamed without proof in a public arena we sue. You'll be hearing from my lawyer.'

'I'll look forward to it,' said McLeod. 'In the meantime, would you like to add weight to your protestations of innocence by agreeing to have your pockets searched?'

'I'll do no such thing.' With a speed that belied her age, Elizabeth leapt off the podium, but she was not quick enough for the FBI agent waiting nearby. The woman conducted a rapid and very public search, rewarded with a button-sized black object. As she handed it to McLeod, Elizabeth was led away in handcuffs, making animal screeches.

Once the din had subsided, McLeod took the remaining members of the ground jury into a private room and explained in his quiet, authoritative way that what he was holding was a remote control. From her judge's seat, Elizabeth had been able to set off the flash at the exact moment it was likely to be most effective.

The aim of her and her accomplices had been to cause Storm to refuse the jump if he looked likely to go clear so that their chosen rider, Blake Tetherington, could come out on top.

'They were trying to fix the result – is that what you're saying?' demanded Susan Hyde, who'd become chairman of the ground jury by default. 'I don't understand. What did they hope to gain?'

'In sports like cricket and football, it's what's known as match fixing,' McLeod said. 'Criminals will place bets of tens of thousands on one team, and then pay referees or players on the opposite team to deliberately lose a match so that they can collect a fortune.

'It's early days in our investigation, but we believe that our chief suspects might have influenced the result of both Wimbledon and the Tour de France, plus two major football matches. In the case of individual sports like eventing, they achieved their aims by blackmailing vulnerable teenage athletes who had a point of weakness. For poor Casey, it was her ex-convict father.'

Five minutes later, the judges returned to the media centre, where the rumour mill had gone ballistic. As reporters and several near-hysterical riders fired questions, Susan Hyde appealed for calm.

'Folks, we are dealing with a unique crisis. In my

thirty-one years of judging, I've never come across another quite like it. Please bear with us. What I can tell you is that, subject to the veterinary check finding Storm Warning sound, we are prepared to offer Casey Blue the chance to ride the round a second time. For obvious reasons, she could not merely jump the final obstacle. She needs to clear all sixteen jumping efforts in the best time, just like her fellow competitors. If she refuses, or if her horse is injured or too tired to perform, I'm afraid the elimination will stand.'

'But what about Don Alexander?' Peter asked McLeod as they left the media centre. 'Now that we know for certain his mother-in-law is involved in the plot, surely that proves he is too? We need to find him. If your theory is right and it was he who attacked Casey at White Oaks, wearing a mask or something, then he's a violent, dangerous man with no conscience. He might try to take revenge on Casey.'

McLeod's face was grim. 'My guess is that he's already on the run. After all, if he's involved in the plot against Casey, he's linked by association to the raid on the art warehouse where the security guard died. So is Chief Superintendent Grady. And now that we have proof that Roland is innocent, we'll be looking at new suspects in the shooting of the security guard.

'As I speak, the FBI and local police are combing the park for Don Alexander. They'll have a job to find him. He's cunning, highly intelligent and well-versed in police search tactics. He might even be in disguise again.

As pleased as I am that Casey has been given a second chance at the title, we're going to have to be vigilant. If he has a chance to finish what he started, he might take it.'

24

A ND SO IT was that at 3.45 p.m., Storm Warning
cantered into the stadium wearing a red fly veil
over his ears that muffled the roar of the crowd and made
him look like the glorious steed of a heroic knight. In
a sense he was, although in place of a medieval warrior
he carried a slender girl with gentle hands and an
intense gaze the colour of the thunderclouds rolling in
overhead.

In an ideal world, Storm would have bolted out into
one of the lush pastures nearby and rolled luxuriously
in the grass. His body was weary. As much as he loved
to gallop and jump, the heat and exertion and the long,
strange journey that began this adventure had sapped
his strength. All he wanted now was to go home.

First, though, he would do this thing for the girl he loved. He had let her down by swerving away from the blinding light at the last jump and she'd fallen hard. She'd pretended to everyone that she was uninjured, but Storm and the old woman knew differently.

In the privacy of his stable, they'd argued over it. Mrs Smith had berated Casey, saying the madness had to stop. She said that no title was worth riding with a cracked collarbone or 'whatever the hell' was wrong with Casey, and what would she achieve anyway? She'd be like a bird trying to fly with a broken wing.

Casey had retorted that it was Storm who'd be doing the flying, and that surely the whole point of the training they'd been doing was using invisible aids. 'I'll use my legs and my voice. Storm will do the rest.'

So here he was, summoning up his last reserves of strength and energy to do her proud. He circled the stadium in a collected canter, neck arched, waiting for the bell that would be his signal to start. But as he passed a rippling green and gold banner, Storm caught a scent that filled him with terror and rage. It was the smell of the man who'd tried to attack him at White Oaks

Scenting him now, Storm veered in his direction, ears pinned to his head. Fortunately or unfortunately, the man was saved by the bell. As Casey's legs closed around his sides, Storm turned away reluctantly and focused on the job in hand. His blood was up. Adrenalin charged around his body like rocket fuel.

When Storm swerved towards a sponsor's banner, Casey was nearly unseated. She was forced to grab at his mane to save herself, and the resulting jolt to her already injured shoulder was so agonising that she let out a small scream. A numbness crept along the limb. She reeled in the saddle, light-headed.

Up in the stands, the spectators heaved a collective sigh as she regained her balance. They knew none of the details of the soap opera that had unfolded behind the scenes, only that foul play was suspected and that a British detective and the FBI had become involved.

On top of that, one of the judges had been replaced at short notice. The announcement hinted at illness. The same judge had apparently fainted between dressage tests on the Friday. But the rumour leaned towards impending disgrace.

By the time Casey Blue entered the arena, frenzied speculation had it that a crazed assassin had tried to kill her and was on the loose, poised to try again. Some people shifted nervously in their seats, looking sideways at their neighbours. Others imagined themselves as have-a-go heroes, rescuing eventing's favourite teenager.

But most saved their anxiety for the thunderstorm closing in overhead. The sky was the colour of bruised plums and speckled black with fleeing birds. An ill wind had begun to swirl. Casey's re-jump promised to be the drama to end all dramas. It would be a shame if it were delayed or, worse still, cancelled altogether.

Below them, the gleaming silver coat of Storm Warning seemed to echo the faraway shivers of lightning as he sailed over the first jump. The rain arrived, perfumed by iron. He tossed his head as it threatened to blur his vision. There was a clatter as he knocked the second fence, the Keeneland post and rails. Impossibly, the rail wobbled and stayed where it was.

The tension was more than many could bear. A crack of thunder made several thousand people jump. Peter, who was watching from the rider's tunnel, spent so much time with his eyes closed that McLeod kept up a running commentary.

'Casey and Storm are over the wall by the skin of their teeth, but to be honest with you they're not looking good. The rain is coming down pretty hard now and it must be playing havoc with Storm's ability to judge distance. He's having to rely on Casey to guide him and she's not in the best shape herself. She's riding with one hand; the other arm is sort of resting on the saddle as if it's broken. She must have damaged it in her fall. Oh no. Oh no!'

'What?' cried Peter. 'What?'

'It's all right. She almost went the wrong way, but corrected herself in the nick of time. They're over the seventh. Now I'm regretting not going for a medical check-up last month. This could easily induce a cardiac arrest. Oh no. Oh no!'

'What now?'

'Why don't you open your eyes and see for yourself? Storm seemed to slip on take-off on the last section of the combination and had to do a sort of corkscrew twist to scramble over. He rolled the pole and somehow, in defiance of gravity and logic, it stayed in the cup. One more fence to go – the thirteenth. Let's hope that this time it's lucky.'

Peter forced himself to watch. He wanted to will Casey to succeed. After that, he'd leave. The cab was booked and waiting. He'd made it a condition of accompanying McLeod to the US, that he be on the first flight out of Kentucky as soon as he knew she was safe. The detective had done his best to talk him out of it, but Peter's mind was made up. One more jump and he'd be gone.

The rain was coming down in sheets. It was hard to tell where it ended and the silver horse began. The elegant show jumping jacket made for Casey by her dad was clinging to her slim, strong body as she bent low over Storm's neck. In her pocket, he knew she'd be carrying the rose brooch that had once belonged to her mother. She seldom rode without it.

Storm cantered towards the jump. *You can do it, boy*, Peter thought. His fists were clenched with nerves. *You can do it.*

Casey laid her palm flat on Storm's neck. It meant that he could trust her the way she trusted him. It meant that it was safe for him to follow her to the ends of the earth. He tucked up his feet and soared.

207

Wild cheers rang out across the stadium. Casey was drenched but laughing as she did a celebratory lap, punching the air in triumph with her good arm. In amid the chaos Peter heard the same words over and over: history, record books, a chance at the Grand Slam.

After Casey had been rather painfully embraced by Mrs Smith and seemingly half the officials and spectators in the stadium (the paramedics kept trying to fight everyone off so they could tend to her injured arm), she emerged to find McLeod leaning patiently against the collecting ring gate. To her disappointment, he was on his own.

'I gather from Mrs Smith that I owe you everything,' she said. 'My father and I will never forget what you've done for us. Please allow me to do something for you in return. Mrs Smith tells me you have a Morgan mare and might be looking for a new livery yard. She texted Morag, the manager at White Oaks, while I was waiting for the vet earlier. There's an empty stable beside Storm's. Any time you want it, it's yours.'

The press officer bustled up, bent under a vast golf umbrella. 'Congrats, Casey. Astonishing result. More twists and drama than a thriller. That a respected judge and possibly a policeman were involved defies belief. And all because of a bet, I hear. Shocking. As you can imagine, the reporters are champing at the bit for your reaction. Would you mind coming with me?'

'Sure,' Casey said, cradling her injured arm. 'No

problem. It's just that there's someone I need to see urgently.'

'Who's that?'

'The boy I love.' She turned to McLeod. 'Where's Peter? I need to see Peter.'

But the young farrier was long gone.

25

'WINDOW, MIDDLE OR aisle?'

Peter snapped out of the haze of misery he'd been in since leaving the Kentucky Horse Park. His head throbbed. 'Excuse me?'

The woman at the check-in counter glanced up for the first time since he'd handed her his passport and became a lot perkier at the sight of him. 'Window, middle or aisle seat. Any preference?'

'I don't mind. I mean, whatever's easiest.'

'What's easiest is if you go,' said a voice from behind him. 'What's best is if you stay.'

Peter turned slowly. A rain-drenched Casey was standing before him, still in her mud-stained breeches, long boots and wet shirt. A sling supported her right arm. Her dark hair hung in dripping ringlets and her grey eyes, with the ring of sky blue around the pupils, were huge in her pale face. A raindrop, or perhaps it was a tear, was suspended on her cheek.

'Best for who?'

'Best for me.' There was a pause and she said hopefully: 'I'd like it to be good for you too.'

He lifted his passport and boarding pass from the desk and avoided the gaze of the check-in woman. 'Thanks.'

'No problem. Enjoy your flight.'

A puddle was forming at Casey's feet.

'What's best for me is to fly back to the UK and go back to work and move on with my life,' Peter said. 'What's best for me is to forget that any of this ever happened. We should have stayed friends. We had a good thing going and we should never have crossed the line. Now we don't even have that.'

He looked at his watch. 'I have to go. I still have to get through security. Casey, I'm happy for you. What you did out there today was unbelievable. You and Storm, you deserve all the glory you get. Watching you jump today was nothing short of magical.'

'You did that,' Casey told him. 'You're responsible for that magic. If you hadn't persuaded McLeod to take the case, Dad wouldn't be free and Storm and I would be on our way home now, having achieved absolutely nothing. If you don't care about me, why did you do it?'

People were starting to stare. Peter slung his bag over his shoulder and moved in the direction of the departures gate. 'I didn't say I didn't care, but that wasn't the reason I did it. I did it because it was the right thing to do. I did it because a serious miscarriage of justice was about to take place and I wasn't going to stand by and watch it happen. If I made any kind of difference, I'm glad.'

He glanced up at the departure board. 'I have to run. Case, go back to the Horse Park and celebrate with Mrs Smith and the other riders. You and I, we can still be mates. We can catch up over a coffee some time.'

Casey looked stricken. 'So that's it. This is goodbye?'

His smile was sad. 'I suppose it is.'

The milling crowd had almost swallowed him when Casey shouted after him: 'Has anyone ever told you that you're extremely stubborn?'

He didn't turn and didn't answer. Casey could barely see the top of his head. In another minute he'd be gone and it would be too late. For the rest of her life, she'd regret not doing what she'd promised herself she'd do – tell him how she felt.

In the distance, Peter moved closer to the conveyor belt sucking hand luggage into the X-ray machine. Casey broke into a run. 'Peter, wait.'

But everyone and everything conspired to block her path and when she reached the departures gate he was nowhere to be seen. She blinked, afraid to believe the evidence of her own eyes.

She turned away and began to make her way slowly through the crowds. Tears poured down her face.

'Hey, didn't you just win the Kentucky Three-Day

Event?' blustered a grinning man in a Stetson. 'What's there to cry about?' His wife dragged him away.

Then all of a sudden Peter was in front of her, holding out a Kleenex. Shielding her from onlookers, he led her out of the airport. They stood beneath an empty bus shelter, looking everywhere but at each other. The rain had stopped and the sun was making rainbows in the puddles on the pavement.

Casey wiped her eyes. She was embarrassed. 'I thought you'd gone.'

'I couldn't. Leave, I mean. There was too much left unsaid.'

'The unsaid things, they're all my fault. I don't find it easy to say how I feel. Sometimes I think that riding is the only way I can really express myself.'

'That's okay,' Peter said gently. 'I understand. I really do.'

'No, it's not okay. It's the opposite of okay. Anyhow, I've made a fool of myself now so I might as well continue. Look, you can go back to Wales if that's what you really want, but if you change your mind in the next five minutes – or ever, if you change your mind ever – there's this wet, muddy and totally exhausted girl who loves you with all her heart.'

'This girl, does she have a name?'

'It's me, silly. *I* love you. I think a part of me loved you from the first moment I saw you, I was just too proud to admit it. I'm so sorry. I wish I'd told you earlier. And now I guess it's much too late.'

He grinned as he gazed down at her. 'Better late than never. I'm not sure I could have survived that. I love you too, Casey Blue. I just didn't know if you felt the same. I thought you'd be better off without me.'

'Well, you were wrong. I need you, Peter Rhys, and I especially need ...'

'What?'

She stood on tiptoes and pressed her mouth to his. 'This.'

If kissing Casey for the first time had been the single best moment of Peter's life, kissing her for the second time topped it.

When they finally broke apart, he kept his arms around her waist, afraid to let her go. 'What happens next – apart, that is, from finding you some dry clothes?'

'First, we should probably let the airline know that you're not going to be taking your flight.' She smiled shyly. 'Then I'm hoping you're going to kiss me again, perhaps somewhere a bit more private. After that, I believe we have some celebrating to do.'

He laughed. 'And after that, there'll be Burghley to look forward to and a chance at the Grand Slam. If we're together, the sky's the limit.'

'Oh, I don't know about that,' said Casey. 'We could always aim a bit higher. What's that old saying? "Next stop the moon."'

Acknowledgments

Writing the *One Dollar Horse* series has been among the most wonderful experiences of my life. For me, there is a particular joy in spending hours of every day immersed in the world of eventing. However, researching this book had particular challenges and for the solution of them I'm indebted to Vanessa Bee, founder of the International Horse Agility Club, and George Mitchell, possibly the finest fitness expert in the UK.

To the one and only Jilly Cooper, author of what must surely be the most wickedly enjoyable horse book ever written, a thousand thanks for the generous acknowledgement and kind words. I hope our paths cross again.

A big thanks also to my agent, Catherine Clarke, my

publicist, Alex Hippisley-Cox and to everyone at Orion Children's Books, especially my editor, Fiona Kennedy, Susan Lamb, Lisa Milton, Jo Carpenter, Jane Hughes, Nina Douglas, Louise Court, Fliss Johnston, Alexandra Nicholas and Sarah Vanden-Abeele. For Jue, thanks seems inadequate but I mean it with all my heart.